THE SOLDIER'S STEADFAST BRIDE

A BLUSHING BRIDES MARRIAGE OF CONVENIENCE ROMANCE

LORANA HOOPES

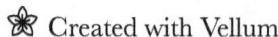

HEIDI

"So, here is what I was thinking. We could open this huge taproom and have all kinds of beers. Imported ones are my favorite, but there's nothing wrong with domestic too."

Heidi stared at the man across from her, unsure how to form the words racing through her mind. "Um, I'm sorry, but I thought this was a date?" She gestured to the restaurant around them. The linen clad tables, the soft lighting. She'd thought this guy at least had potential. He wasn't her normal type, but unlike a few of the others, at least he had a full head of hair and relatively straight teeth.

His smile though was a different story. It was wide and eager, like a kid blowing out candles on his birthday cake, but somehow it reminded Heidi more of the joker than a happy kid. "I know, but what better way to pass the time before our food comes than to discuss our future."

"Our future? What future?" Heidi blinked as she tried to grapple with what was happening here. "We just met. This is our first date. First." And probably last, she thought, but there was no need to say that aloud.

His hand snaked across the table and grasped hers. "The first of many, I hope. We have so much in common. You love wine. I love beer. Together, we could have a spirited future." He grinned even wider. "Did you like that play on words? Ooh, maybe we could call our taproom that."

A feeling of revulsion shot through Heidi as she glanced down at his hand on hers, but before she could react, he pulled his hand back and leaned over to the satchel he had evidently brought in before she arrived. That little treasure he had kept hidden under the table until the order was placed and it was too late for Heidi to run screaming for the hills. Then, he'd nonchalantly brought out pamphlets from some of his favorite taprooms. At first, she'd thought he was trying to convince her to have their second date at one, but now she was no longer sure what was happening. Only that she had gotten on an elevator to Crazy town that appeared to have no stop button and no top floor.

"I drew up a business proposal that I think your

parents will find highly lucrative," he continued as he rummaged in the satchel.

Heidi's forehead wrinkled in confusion. "My parents? What are you talking about?"

His face reappeared along with a large stack of papers in his hand which he slid across the table. "Of course your parents will have to be involved unless they've left you the money. I'm sorry, I just figured that a preschool teacher wouldn't have the disposable capital to invest in a taproom."

"Of course I don't have that kind of capital, but neither do my parents. Did you think they would just jump on a chance to finance the taproom of some man they haven't even met?" Anger was building in Heidi's stomach, quickly morphing into a tumultuous ball of fire.

Ian, if that was even his name, sat back and pushed his glasses up the bridge of his nose. It was sharp, too sharp now that she was taking the time to really observe him. It reminded her of a skewer, and she had to press her lips together to keep from laughing out loud.

Ian folded his arms across his chest. "Well, I won't be a stranger once you introduce us."

"Is this why you reached out to me?" Heidi had suffered her fair share of crazy dates ever since she'd returned from the reality TV show Who Wants to Marry a Cowboy, but this guy was quickly taking the cake for the craziest of them all.

His features softened and his face took on the condescending expression of someone trying to explain something to a child. "Of course not," he began, reaching for her hand once again. She pulled it out of his reach and clasped it tightly with her other hand, planting both of them firmly in her lap and as far from him as she could get them. The action didn't seem to deter him. "I wanted to meet you because you are so beautiful and kind and because we have so much in common."

"What do we have in common?" Heidi asked. "We don't even like the same drinks. I like wine and you prefer beer. I teach preschool and you…" She faltered when she realized she didn't even know what he did. "What do you even do?"

"I'm a computer analyst for a leading software company. I've been saving every penny, and maybe we won't even need your parents' money, but their capital could get this started much sooner. Otherwise, it will be at least another year before I can even begin looking for a place."

"My parents aren't going to finance anything." Heidi had tried her best to keep calm, but this was all too much. Why did this man, whom she'd just met a few days ago, think she would want to open a business with him?

His face fell. "Oh, well, are you sure? You haven't looked at the business proposal yet. It's very sound, and

I'm sure if you show it to them, they will be inclined to agree."

"Are you listening to me? They won't agree because they don't know you and because they don't like beer. We own a vineyard, that's it." She threw her hands up in frustration. "You know what? I don't normally leave a date after the food has been ordered because I think it's rude, but I'm afraid I'll have to make an exception in your case."

Before he could say another word, Heidi grabbed her purse, stood, and exited the restaurant. That was it. She was giving up men and dating. At least until the next season of the show came out and people forgot all about her. She had never wanted to be the center of attention - she still wasn't even sure why she'd agreed to that show - but ever since she'd returned home, she'd had one dating proposal after another. Inclined to believe that at least a few of them had to have redeeming qualities, she had accepted only to realize that most of them cared more about the fleeting fame and what she could do for them than about her.

With a frustrated sigh, she slid into her car and pointed it away from the restaurant. She wasn't ready to go home yet though, so she was unsurprised when she found herself on the well-traveled path to her best friend, Linley's house.

Linley was almost the exact opposite of Heidi which was probably why they worked so well as friends. Where

Heidi had red hair, Linley's was dark brown. Where Heidi preferred a few close friends and a quiet evening, Linley enjoyed dancing and crowds of people. However, they were both teachers, and they had bonded over their love of children.

"Whoa, what happened?" Linley asked when she opened the front door ten minutes later.

Heidi stumbled into the familiar living room and fell into the soft sofa before dropping her head into her hands. "I can't do it anymore. I just can't."

Linley chuckled as she sat down in the antique rocking chair closest to the couch. "What are you talking about?"

"Dating." Heidi lifted her head and tucked her hair behind her ears. Her eyes fell to the cup of tea sitting on the table between them. From the tiny wisps of steam dancing above it, she could tell it was still warm, and she was tempted to ask for one for herself. "It's awful. Ever since I appeared on that reality TV show, men have been coming out of the woodwork."

Linley lifted a perfectly manicured brow. "Most women would kill for that problem, you know."

"I know," Heidi groaned, "and that's what makes it worse, but they are just... just..." she paused, searching for the right words, "not what I'm looking for. This date I just left? He showed up with a business proposal for a taproom which was tacky enough, but when I reminded him that my parents owned a vineyard and only dealt with wine, he wouldn't even take no for an answer. He just continued the proposal as if that didn't matter."

Linley picked up the cup and blew on it softly. "Okay, well there's bound to be a few duds in the mix, but surely there have been a few men you'd like to see again?" Linley had a habit of always looking at the bright side of things which Heidi normally loved. Heck, it was a trait they normally shared, but right now, she didn't want to see the bright side. What she wanted was to commiserate with her friend and wallow in self-pity.

"Um, well let me see. There was Doug who plays for the minor league hockey team and only had half of his original teeth left." A grimace flashed across Linley's face, but Heidi didn't stop. "Then there was Ned, the beekeeper, who carried a pager in case there was a bee emergency." She ticked the men off on her fingers. "And, of course, who could forget Brick? The sweet southern gentleman who wanted to dress me up as a Belle, call me some sort of a flower, and move me back to Alabama?"

Linley nodded and mashed her lips together to keep from smiling. "Perhaps reality TV was not quite the fame you were looking for."

Heidi threw her hands up in the air. "I wasn't looking for fame at all. I was looking for love."

Linley reached across the table and placed a hand on Heidi's. "I know. We all want love, but sometimes it's about waiting on God's timing."

"I know. That's what Tyler said too, but I'm not getting any younger." Her stomach emitted an inopportune growl at that moment causing both girls to giggle.

"Guess you're not getting any fuller either," Linley said with a smile. "Did you skip out before eating?"

Heidi rolled her eyes at her friend. "Did you not just hear my story? The man wanted to open a taproom with me."

"Right, well, I think there's some spaghetti left. Why don't you help yourself and eat your cares away? Everything looks better after a plate of spaghetti, right?"

Heidi sighed, but a smile flitted across her lips. The spaghetti would take care of the ache in her stomach, but chatting with Linley was definitely a better cure for everything else that ailed her. Except for her lonely heart. Even Linley couldn't cure that.

2

CORY

a vice-like feeling squeezed Cory's heart as he stared at the letter in his hand. This couldn't be happening. They had promised not to deploy him after Desiree died. Or at least not until he could make sure to have arrangements for Bella.

A hand clapped his shoulder, dragging his attention away from the foreboding words on the innocuous piece of paper. "What's the matter, man?" His best friend, Tanner, stared at him with a raised brow. "You look like you've seen a ghost."

With a sigh, Cory held the letter out for him to see. Tanner took the paper and quickly scanned it, his eyes widening as he neared the bottom. "I thought you said they promised to work with you."

"They did." He snatched the paper back. "I guess they

changed their minds." He should be used to it by now. The Army was notorious for saying one thing and doing another. It was how he had ended up in Washington state as it was. He and Desiree had asked for a station in Italy in order to be closer to his aging parents, and the Army had promised they would accommodate him, but at the last minute, they had sent them to Washington state instead. They'd claimed it was because the person he was going to replace was promoted and therefore able to stay at the base in Italy, nullifying the job opening, but it hadn't made Desiree any happier.

"So, what are you going to do?" Tanner asked, leaning against the desk.

"I have no idea. I don't have time to take Bella to Italy, and even if I could, my parents are too old to take care of her. I don't have any brothers or sisters to help out. Desiree's parents both passed away years ago, and her sister already has a huge family to take care of." Cory ran a hand over his close-cropped hair in frustration. "Maybe I can appeal?"

Appeals did exist but not only did they take a while, they were generally used for medical emergencies. He'd never heard of anyone getting an appeal due to a childcare issue, but then he'd never known anyone in his situation. Was it even possible?

"What about a close friend? I know it's not perfect, and there's probably some red tape-"

Cory cut him off. "I'm not leaving Bella with a friend for six months."

Tanner tapped a finger against his lips. "Wait," he said, a spark flashing in his eyes, "what about that girl you were talking about the other night?"

Cory tried to rein in his wandering mind and focus on what Tanner was saying. "What girl?"

"The one on that show we were watching…" Tanner snapped his fingers as if trying to remember the name of it. Then his face lit up. "That reality dating show about marrying a cowboy."

Neither Tanner nor Cory normally watched reality dating shows, but they'd been stuck on shift with Sarah, a fellow soldier who did, and a few minutes into the show, Cory had realized he'd gone to high school with one of the contestants. After Sarah had realized this, she'd goaded him into watching to see how Heidi did. Unfortunately, she hadn't made it to the end, but he'd enjoyed seeing her again, even if it was only on the TV screen.

"Heidi?" he asked, finally answering Tanner.

Tanner smiled and pointed at him. "That's the one. Didn't you say you guys were friends in high school?"

Cory shook his head in disbelief; Tanner must have lost his mind. "Yeah, but I can't just call up an old classmate and ask her to take on my daughter for six months."

A mischievous smile tugged at Tanner's lips. "Yeah, that would be weird, except didn't you tell me that you two made a pact in high school?"

Cory clamped his lips together as the realization of Tanner's innuendo sank in. That had been a long time ago, and he never should have told Tanner about it. "It was high school, man. That was over ten years ago."

"Yeah, well, she's obviously still single, and you are now single…" He lifted his eyebrows to finish his thought.

"True, but I can't just show up and dump that on her. Plus, I was married, so technically I don't think that counts."

Even as he dismissed the idea to Tanner, he couldn't stop turning it over in his head. Heidi had been his best friend in high school. Yes, they had lost touch when he'd graduated, but she'd always been there for him before. Plus, she was a teacher which meant she was probably good with kids, and she had gone on the show which should mean that not only was she single but that she was looking for a relationship. He wasn't sure he could offer her love - his heart was still with Desiree - but he could at least offer her security and fidelity. Would that be enough for her though?

Tanner folded his arms and fixed Cory with an even stare. "I don't see that you have much choice. At least try and talk to her. The worst that can happen is that she'll say no and you'll be right back where you are now, but what if she says yes?"

Cory opened his mouth to reply, but Tanner was right. His options were limited. He could try for an appeal, but he had no idea how long that might take or if they would even grant it. The date of the deployment probably wasn't going to get delayed which left him with about thirty days to find someone to watch Bella, and right now, Heidi was his best shot.

"Okay, I'll try."

3

HEIDI

*H*eidi finished the last bulletin board and stepped back to appraise it. Pretty good if she did say so herself. This was her favorite bulletin board. It was the one that held a giant calendar with tiny Velcro pieces on each day and apples around the side numbered for each day of the month. Once she taught the lesson on numbers and days of the week, the children would take turns placing the correct apple on the appropriate day. It was a board she had started her first year of teaching and continued every year as the children seemed to enjoy it as much as she did.

Decorating for the beginning of school was one of her favorite things about fall. She also loved the changing colors, the cooler temperatures, and the falling leaves, but there was something about bringing the color into her room that always brightened her day. And when the children entered and oohed and aahed, she knew she'd done a good job.

"Knock, Knock."

Heidi turned toward the vaguely familiar masculine voice and nearly dropped her stapler. "Cory? Cory Kingman?" Though she hadn't seen him in years, she was fairly certain the man standing in her doorway was her friend from high school, and he was as handsome as ever.

"Hey, Heidi," he said as he stepped toward her, "I hope you don't mind me stopping by. The ladies in the office said it would be okay."

"Mind?" She placed the stapler on her desk before hurrying to him and throwing her arms around him. "Why would I mind?"

He returned her hug with a slight laugh. "Well, it has been a few years. I wasn't even sure you'd remember me."

"Remember you?" She pulled back but kept her hands on his shoulders. "How could I forget my debate partner and best friend?"

In truth, she had once wanted more, but he'd made it very clear that he saw her more like a little sister than a love interest, so she'd settled for what she could. When he'd graduated a year before she had, they had gradually lost touch though she'd heard through the grapevine that he'd joined the military.

"It's so good to see you, but what are you doing here?"

A shadow flitted across his face before being replaced with a smile. "Well, I actually live here now."

"You do?" She dropped her hands and took a step back though she didn't want to. However, she didn't want anything to appear inappropriate in her classroom. This job was too important to her. "Why have we not met up before?"

"Well, I work at the base up the road, but I didn't know you lived here until I saw you on the show."

Heidi cringed and shook her head. "Ah, the show. Not the brightest idea I've ever had. I can't believe you actually watch that show."

"I don't, normally," he said with a chuckle, "but a girl I work with does. Once she found out I knew you, she kept me informed on the show."

Heidi let out a wry chuckle. "Well, finding you again is about the best thing to come from going on that show. At least it wasn't a total waste."

"Not a great experience, I take it?"

"Not in the least." Heidi shook her head and took a step back to lean on a desk. "Not only was the experience slightly embarrassing, but men have been coming out of the woodwork to date me since I returned. And not the kind you want to date."

"I'm sorry to hear that." He chewed on his bottom lip for a moment as if he wanted to say more but wasn't sure if it was a good idea. "Well, I'd love to take you to lunch if you have time to take a break."

Heidi glanced around the room. She did still have some work to do, but she could probably take a few hours off and still finish without having to stay too late. Besides, it was Cory. Not only had she missed him, but she wasn't sure when she would have another opportunity to hang out with him.

"I'd like that," she said with a smile.

After grabbing her purse from her desk, she led the way to the front office to tell her boss where she was going. Then, they exited the school together. "Your car or mine?" she asked as they stepped into the parking lot.

"I'll drive," he said, shaking his keys. "As long as you don't mind a slightly crunchy floor. It seems that no matter how many times I clean, my daughter finds a way to drop crumbs."

Heidi paused and touched his arm to still him. "I didn't know you had a daughter. Are you sure your wife would be okay with us going to lunch?" Though she wanted to see her old friend, she had no desire to get in the middle of a marriage.

Cory's face fell. "My wife died a year ago, so there's no worry there."

"Cory, I'm so sorry. I didn't know." Empathy flooded Heidi, but she'd never been married, much less lost someone so close to her, so she wasn't sure exactly what to say.

He shook his head once. "It's okay. It is what it is, but let's not let that gray cloud hang over our lunch."

"If you say so." It was clear that Cory was still grieving, but Heidi wasn't going to press the issue.

The drive to the restaurant was silent and almost uncomfortable, but Cory's mood seemed to change as they entered the quaint deli.

"I hope you don't mind me picking, but I love this place," Cory said as he led the way to a table by the window.

"Not at all." Heidi smiled up at him as he held out her seat for her. "It's actually one of my favorite places too."

In fact, the deli was one she frequented often on staff development days. Not only was it close, but she loved the homey atmosphere of the place. A sweet, elderly German couple ran it, and they had filled the place with German charm. The walls were painted in bright murals depicting idyllic German towns and even the staff dressed in Lederhosen and Bavarian outfits.

"You know this is pretty accurate," Cory said as he opened his menu.

"The deli?" Heidi asked. "I know. I've been to Germany a few times with my parents. In fact, there's this little place in Landstuhl-"

"Andreas Stube," he finished for her with a smile. "I loved that place. I ate there a lot when I was stationed in Germany."

"I didn't know you were stationed there," Heidi said. Of course she shouldn't be surprised. She didn't know much about Cory's life after he left high school.

"Yep, for four years. It was amazing, although harder to stay in shape with all the fried foods."

Heidi chuckled. She remembered well the five pounds she had gained after their weekend excursion in Germany a few years back. "I can imagine. I only spent a weekend there, but I ended up having to work off what I gained for the next month. I'm not sure I could actually live there."

"It took some adjusting to, that's for sure, but I do miss it now and then. However, I do have to say Washington weather is pretty similar to Germany's."

"So, where else have you been?" Heidi asked as she glanced down at her menu. She was fairly certain she knew what she wanted, but it never hurt to see if they had added anything new.

"Well, after high school, I was stationed in California for a few years. Then, I got transferred to Germany for four years. Then Texas, South Carolina, and finally back here."

"Wow, you've been around." Heidi couldn't imagine moving that much. True, there were times she thought about leaving Washington, especially for a more conservative state where she didn't feel vilified for her religious beliefs, but traveling with her parents seemed to quiet those urges. At least for now.

A wry chuckle tumbled from his lips. "Kind of a hazard with the Army. They like to keep you moving every few years. It's nice to see so many new places, but it's hard on family. I'm hoping I can stay here for a few years, so Bella can put down some roots."

"Bella is your daughter?" Heidi was curious about his daughter, and his late wife, but she didn't want him to think she was nosy or prying.

Cory grinned, and his eyes lit up. "Yep. Bella is five and a handful. Such a girly girl and way too smart for her own good."

"Well, I'm sure she got some of that from you," Heidi said, matching his smile. "I seem to recall you being a pretty bright cookie, at least when it came to debate."

His smile faltered, and the light slipped out of his eyes. "I can't take all the credit for her intelligence. Desiree was a huge part of how she turned out as well."

"I'm sure she was." A heavy silence fell between them, and while Heidi was desperate to lift it, she wasn't sure how. Relief flooded her when the waitress approached and took their order.

"So, what about you," Cory said, changing the subject

after the waitress left. His voice was still strained, but Heidi could tell that he was trying to lighten the mood again, and she appreciated it. "What have you been up to for the last decade?"

4

CORY

"Well, my story isn't as exciting as yours, I'm afraid," Heidi said, before pausing to take a sip of her water. "After high school, I attended college where I earned my teaching degree. Then I came back here, and I've been teaching preschool ever since."

"I'm sure that comes with its fair share of interesting stories." Cory chuckled softly. He could write a book on all the funny things Bella had done, and she was only one child.

"True, it does, but other than that, my life has been pretty boring. Going on that silly reality show was the highlight of my excitement, and I rather wish I hadn't done it now." Heidi rolled her eyes and took a sip of her water.

Cory cocked his head and studied her for a moment.

"Why did you go on the show?" In fact, he wondered how she was still single. Heidi was beautiful with her auburn hair and creamy skin, and she was sweet as well. Why hadn't a good man snatched her up already? Of course, while he was curious, that wasn't the question he really wanted to ask, but he couldn't just throw that question at her. Better to work up to it.

Heidi sighed and twirled a strand of her auburn hair around her finger. "I don't know. All of my friends are married or are getting married, and I'm still alone. I always thought I would be married by now with a kid of my own - like you."

He smiled and nodded. This was his opening, but was it too early? Only one way to find out. "Would you still like to? Be married that is?"

Heidi blinked at him as if he'd spoken in a foreign language. "Um, I guess, but in case it wasn't clear, there isn't even anyone on the radar right now."

Cory chuckled. "But if there was someone on the radar, you wouldn't be opposed to marriage?"

Heidi narrowed her eyes at Cory. "What exactly are you getting at, Cory?"

He bit the inside of his lip as he studied her face. Was he really going to jump down this rabbit hole? He'd brought her here for that reason; he might as well go through with it. He decided to spit the words out quickly, like ripping off a Band-Aid. "Do you remember that pact we made in high school?" And there it was. Out in the open. No taking it back now.

Tiny lines sprouted on Heidi's forehead as her brow furrowed. Did she not remember the pact? Then, suddenly, as her eyes widened, he knew that she did. "Wait, do you mean the one where we promised to marry each other if neither of us were married by the age of thirty?"

"That is the one to which I'm referring. Unless you made some other pacts in high school that I didn't know about."

Heidi chuckled and shook her head. The light from above hit her copper hair and created the illusion of a sparkly halo around her head. "No, that was the only one, but I don't understand. I'm not thirty yet, and you are married, well, a widower, but you know what I mean."

"I do know what you mean." He needed to touch something, focus his attention on anything other than how dry his throat was and how fast his heart was beating. His hand circled his glass, and he turned it slightly as he tried to form the right words. "The truth is, I'm kind of in a bind, and I thought maybe you could help."

He paused and glanced up at her, but she merely blinked at him, waiting for him to finish. "After Desiree died, the Army promised they wouldn't deploy me, at least for a while, because I have no one to take care of Bella. Unfortunately, they seem to have forgotten that promise because I received deployment orders yesterday. I know it's asking a lot, especially since we haven't spoken in years, but I don't have another option."

Heidi stared at him a moment as if she hadn't registered what he was asking which she probably hadn't. He realized he hadn't been that clear.

"What about your parents? Or Desiree's family?"

"Unfortunately, Desiree's parents are deceased and her sister already has a full house. My parents are too elderly, and they live in Italy. That's farther than I want to move Bella. It's going to be an adjustment for her as it is, but sending her across the world just doesn't seem fair."

"But… but I don't even know your daughter. Why would you want to leave her with me?" Heidi's wide eyes brimmed with concern.

Cory held her gaze, hoping she would read his sincerity. "Because I know you, and I trust you."

"But marriage? That's so permanent. Couldn't I just agree to take care of her?"

Cory sighed and shook his head. "Unfortunately, because I'm military, there are things you can't do unless you are a military spouse like taking her to a doctor if necessary. Plus, if anything should happen to me, she would need to be with a direct relative or my spouse."

Heidi sat back and let out a long low sigh. "I don't know what to say, Cory. I want to help, but that's a lot. We were just kids when we made that pact. I didn't think we'd ever actually use it."

"I didn't either, Heidi." He leaned forward, closing the distance between them. "Believe me, this wasn't how I saw my life going, and I know popping into your life and asking this is crazy, but will you at least think about it?"

Her eyes searched his before she finally nodded. "Of course."

Their food arrived then and halted the conversation for a time. When they did speak again, it was on to lighter topics which Cory was glad for. Though he desperately needed Heidi's help, he had also missed his high school friend and was delighted to catch up with her.

"So, I'm not saying I'm agreeing," Heidi said as he paid the bill, "but how exactly did you see this working? Especially since I don't know your daughter. I do, however, know young children, and I know leaving her with a total stranger would not be a good thing."

"No, you're right, it wouldn't." Cory led the way to the exit. "I have thirty days before I deploy. IF you agree, the first thing I would do is get Bella transferred to your school. It is more than a preschool, right? It looked like it was." He opened the door and held it open for her to exit first.

"Yes, we're pre-k through fifth grade. Then we feed into a junior high for sixth through eighth grade, and a high school for beyond that."

"That's what I thought." He paused long enough to open the car door for her and get in the driver's side. "So, I'd get her in school at your building. That way it would be less of a burden on you to take her every day. I know I'm asking a lot, so I'd like to make as many things as easy as I can. The next step would be to introduce the two of you. I'd like her to spend as much time with you as possible before I deploy. It won't solve everything, but it would certainly help. I wish she were older so she would understand more. She has been through a deployment before but she was a lot younger, so I'm not sure how much she remembers. She's also seen some of her friends go through deployments recently, though it's not quite the same. That being said, she'll adjust, and besides I know you, Heidi. And I know you are great with kids."

Heidi nodded as she fastened her seatbelt. "Well, I promise to consider it, but would you be open to me meeting Bella before I give you a final answer?"

Cory bit the inside of his lip to keep from smiling as he started the car. "I think that would be a great idea." Bella was a sweetheart, and Cory felt confident that having Heidi meet her would only strengthen his case.

5

HEIDI

*H*eidi was still in a daze as she returned to her classroom after lunch. It had been so good to see Cory again - she'd forgotten how much she had cared about him at one time - but his proposal still hung over her head. She wanted to help him, and if she was honest with herself, she was still attracted to him, but it was clear that he was still in love with his deceased wife. And why wouldn't he be? The question was, could she marry someone who didn't love her?

Normally the answer to that question would be a resounding no, but this wasn't a normal situation. He had seemed as if he had no other option, and though Heidi had yet to meet the girl, she couldn't imagine how hard it would be to send a five-year-old across the ocean to live in another country.

A knock at her classroom door grabbed her attention, and she turned to see Linley standing in the doorway. "I heard you had a handsome visitor. Care to spill?"

"I'm dying to. Come in and shut the door behind you." Heidi loved that Linley was her best friend, and she especially loved that she worked in the same building and they could chat like this.

Linley's brow lifted, but she shut the door and hurried across the room, snagging a chair close to Heidi's desk to sit in. "Okay, spill."

"The handsome visitor was a friend from high school, my debate partner, Cory Kingman."

"Wait, the Cory Kingman you had a huge crush on in high school?"

Linley hadn't gone to high school with Heidi, but they'd shared stories of their high school years one night over a bucket of ice cream and a woe-is-me session.

"Yes, the same one."

Linley's eyes twinkled, and she leaned closer. "So, is there love in the air? Sparks? Anything?"

"For me? Yes. For him? I don't think so. He actually wanted a favor." Heidi bit the inside of her lip. How would Linley react to Cory's request?

"A favor?" Linley's brows lifted high on her forehead. "What kind of a favor?"

"He wants me to marry him." There was way more to

it than that, but Heidi figured she might as well start with the kicker.

"Um, that's not a favor. It's a proposal. I know you've had a rough patch of dating recently, but I didn't think you'd mistake a proposal."

"It wasn't a real proposal. He's proposing a marriage of convenience."

"What?" The word exploded out of Linley's mouth with such force that Heidi almost felt the word hit her.

Heidi held up her hand to explain. "He's military and a widower with a daughter. Evidently, he received deployment papers and has to find some place for his daughter - someone to take care of her while he's gone."

"What about his own family? Or his wife's family? Surely, he has someone who knows his daughter who can care for her."

They were the same questions that Heidi had asked over their lunch. "Cory is an only child, so he doesn't have any brothers or sisters. His parents are elderly and evidently, they live in Italy. His wife's parents are both deceased, and while she has a sister still living, the sister has a big family already and has no room for Bella." Even as she said the words, she could hear the next question forming in Linley's mind.

"Okay, that's unfortunate, but I still don't see how it's your problem."

Heidi mashed her lips together before taking a deep

breath. "You're right; it's not really, but," she paused and rolled her eyes, "you're going to think I'm nuts, but we made a pact in high school."

Linley folded her arms across her chest. "Yep, I do think you're nuts. A pact? What kind of pact?"

"A pact that we would marry each other if neither of us were married at age thirty." The words sounded so silly when Heidi said them aloud that she could hardly believe she was telling Linley about this.

"But he was married, and you aren't thirty yet."

"I know, but he isn't married now, and I'll be thirty in two months."

"Are you actually considering this?" Linley asked, her head falling forward in shock.

Was she? "I don't know," Heidi said, tucking a strand of hair behind her ear. Her eyes fell to her lap before meeting Linley's again. "Am I crazy if I say yes?"

"Yes, crazy is definitely the word I would use." Linley shook her head. "Why are you considering it? Is it because of the show? Are you afraid you won't find someone? Because that is definitely not the case."

"It's not just that," Heidi said though those doubts definitely resided in her mind. "It's also because he's a friend and because he needs my help. Is it wrong to want to help?"

"No, but do you really want to marry the guy just to help him out? You don't believe in divorce, remember?

What if his daughter is awful? What if you hate being married to him? What if he snores in his sleep or what if he gambles or swears? Do you even know anything about who he is now? He could have changed in the last ten years. I'm sure you have."

Actually, Heidi wasn't sure she had changed much at all, but she could appreciate Linley's concerns. They were valid points and ones Heidi hadn't considered. "You're right," she said with a sigh. "I should find out more about him before I decide. He said he wanted to introduce me to his daughter anyway, so I'll tell him my decision is contingent on how well I get along with his daughter and him as he is now."

"I guess that's a start," Linley said. "I still think you're crazy for even considering this, but you know the man better than I do." She stood and shook her head. "I have to get back to decorating. Even with your lunch break, you have more done than I do. I'll never understand how you're such a decorating whiz."

"You'll get there," Heidi said with a laugh. This was her sixth year of teaching preschool and only Linley's second year of teaching Kindergarten. Some things, like decorating quickly, came with experience, and Heidi had no doubt that Linley would catch up with her soon. "Let me know if you need help. I'll just be finishing up here and contemplating my future."

Linley chuckled as she headed for the door. "Good

luck with that. I can't wait to hear what you decide, but if you do agree to the marriage, I better be a bridesmaid."

Heidi rubbed a hand across the back of her neck. A bridesmaid? She hadn't even thought of the actual wedding. Had his proposal even included an actual wedding? It hadn't included a ring, so perhaps he just expected to do a small ceremony with a justice of the peace. Could she do that? Even though she knew it didn't matter in the long run, the thought of not having an actual wedding was depressing. She wanted one. Even if it was small.

But if she agreed to this and if he agreed to a wedding, would there even be time to plan one? A headache began forming in the back of her mind as a new swarm of questions pushed their way to the front. She needed to decide what she was doing and quickly. She couldn't start the year with her head like this.

6

CORY

Cory pulled into the daycare parking lot with fewer than five minutes to spare. The center was on base, only ten minutes from his work, but that didn't always help when his job ran late, and they had a strict policy of charging him five dollars for every minute they had to watch Bella past closing time.

"Cutting it close again, aren't we Sergeant Kingman?" the lady at the front desk asked as he hurriedly scribbled his name on the sign-out sheet. He thought her name was Nikki, but there were so many women at the center who looked similar that he couldn't be sure and she wasn't wearing a name badge.

"Yes, sorry. Had to finish up with some paperwork before I could get out of there."

"You know the school won't really be able to

accommodate late pickups when she starts there next week. Have you thought about arrangements?"

Cory clenched his jaw and forced a tight smile. He had thought of arrangements, not that they were any of this woman's business, but they also depended on Heidi. He knew it was a lot to ask, but he was hoping, if she agreed to the marriage, that she'd take care of Bella after school until he got home. It would be good practice for when he deployed and she had Bella all the time. What he didn't know was what he was going to do if she said no. "I'm working on it."

The woman nodded, but the set of her lips and her lifted brows told him she didn't believe him. "Well, I hope you do."

"Daddy," Bella called as she emerged from a classroom down the hall. She threw herself at him, and he swung her up in a giant hug.

"Hey, bug," he said, squeezing her tight. She was getting big, and he wouldn't be able to lift her this easily in a few months. In fact, by the time he returned from deployment, she would be nearly a year older. The thought sobered him, and he fought to keep the smile on his face. He didn't want to worry Bella sooner than he had to. "How was your day?"

"It was great. We made scarecrows and pumpkins and leaves and we learned that this season is called fall. I love fall because the leaves are so pretty. Do you love fall too, Daddy?"

Fall was generally his least favorite of the seasons. The pretty leaves she loved so much generally ended up on his front lawn, and he would spend hours in the cold raking them into bags so as not to get dinged by the military police. On top of that, fall was the season Desiree got sick, and the constant reminder of love being in the air and cuddling up with the ones you loved only made him miss her more. But he couldn't say any of that to Bella. "I love you, bug, and that's all that matters," he said instead, setting her back down on the floor and grabbing her coat off the small rack. "Now, what do you say we get some pizza for dinner?"

"Yes," she cheered, thrusting her fist up in the air.

Cory knew pizza wasn't the healthiest dinner, and they probably ate it more than they should, but he wasn't the greatest cook to begin with. Add in the fact that he was exhausted by the time they got home in the evenings, and he just didn't have it in him to cook a fancy meal. He didn't know if Heidi cooked, but he imagined Bella would eat better with her in charge. Teachers got out earlier in the day, didn't they?

He shook his head to clear the thought. He was putting too much hope in the fact that Heidi might agree to this scheme. She would probably say no. In fact, she'd have to be crazy to agree. He'd shown up after nearly a decade of not talking to her and thrown this in her lap. He should have practiced what he was going to say, come up with some compensation or something.

"Daddy, are we going?" Bella tugged on his hand, and he smiled down at her as he tried to push the fears and doubts from his mind.

"Yep, let's go, bug."

His phone rang as he finished buckling Bella into the seat. A glance at the caller ID sent his heart skipping in his chest. It was Heidi. They had exchanged numbers over lunch so they could set up a time for her to meet Bella, but he hadn't expected to hear from her so soon.

"Hello?" He climbed into the driver's side, but waited to insert the key. He didn't need this call going over the car's speaker.

"Cory? It's Heidi although I guess you probably knew that because I'm sure you checked the caller ID." She was rambling, and he couldn't help but smile at the stream of words. It had been her nervous habit in high school and it appeared she hadn't outgrown it yet.

"Yeah, I did, but good to hear from you, Heidi." He paused, unsure if she was calling because she'd made a decision or for some other reason. A part of him wanted to ask and the other part of him was afraid she was calling to tell him no.

"You too. I mean thank you." She exhaled loudly, and he could almost see her shake her head on the other end.

"Anyway, I don't have a decision yet, but I wanted to know when you have time for me to meet Bella. A connection is very important in a situation like this, and while I know you're on a time crunch, I can't really consider it until I make sure that part would be okay. Does that sound awful?"

"Not at all," Cory said with a chuckle. "In fact, what are you doing right now? We were just about to go out for pizza. Would you care to meet us?"

"Now?" Surprise filled her voice, but he hoped it wouldn't keep her from saying yes. "Um, well, I was just planning on eating dinner at home with my cat, but I suppose I could meet you for pizza. Did you have a place in mind?"

"Are you familiar with The Pizza Cafe?" The Pizza Cafe was a small restaurant hidden between a flower shop and a laundromat just outside the base. It didn't look like much from the outside, but it was run by an Italian couple who made the best pizza he'd ever tasted. And he'd tried pizza in a lot of places. They also appealed to young kids with their paper tablecloths that could be colored on and the basket of card games stocked on every table.

"I've never been there, but I've heard about it. Are you heading there now?"

"We are. We're probably closer than you are. Would you like us to wait until you get there to order or do you still like pepperoni and cashews on your pizza?"

A soft chuckle reached his ears through the phone. "I can't believe you remember that."

"It's hard to forget. Nobody else I know likes nuts on their pizza."

He still remembered the first time she'd ordered that combination. It had been after a debate competition, one where they'd taken home the first-place trophy and the other team from their school had placed third. Because of their success, the coach had agreed to take them to a restaurant to celebrate instead of making them eat the food provided at the tournament like normal. Though tournament food wasn't terrible, it was generally put on by the hosting school's cafeteria, so it definitely wasn't the same as dining at a restaurant. They'd stopped at a small pizzeria on the way home, and he'd agreed to split a pizza with her - any one of her choice. He'd had no idea at the time that she liked cashews on pizza. While the sound hadn't appealed to him, he'd been surprised to learn the flavor somehow worked, and while it wasn't his normal choice - he preferred lots of meat - he had found himself ordering it once or twice over the years.

"That is still what I order though you'll be happy to know I also branch out occasionally and add olives or pineapple."

Olives and cashews? Even the sound of that together sent his stomach twisting. "How about we stick with the tried-and-true tonight and save the adventurous stuff for another day?"

"Sounds good," she said with a laugh. "I just googled the place and it looks like it's about twenty minutes for me."

"Okay, we'll meet you there." After a quick goodbye, he ended the call and set the phone down in the passenger seat.

"Who are we meeting, Daddy?" Bella asked from the backseat.

She'd been so quiet that he'd almost forgotten she was back there. He shouldn't have been surprised she was listening intently though. The girl was too smart for her own good sometimes. "We're meeting a friend of mine. A very dear friend."

"Is she my age? Does she like to color?"

Cory chuckled as he started the car. "She is not your age, but I bet she does like to color. She's a teacher." He wondered if she still doodled on things the way she had in high school. More than once, he'd found her handiwork on their debate evidence in the middle of a round. Thankfully, she'd stuck to the sides with her vines and flowers.

"Will she be my teacher?"

"No, I'm afraid not. She teaches kids younger than you, but you might end up going to the school where she works."

"That would be nice, but not as nice as if she were my teacher."

Cory smiled at the simple acceptance of children. Bella didn't even know Heidi, but she had already decided she would like the woman. It was the same with children her own age. Every park they went to, Bella made a friend before they went home. It didn't matter what color the child was or age or gender. More than once, Cory had watched her and wished adults could be more like kids in that way. Too much in the world today centered around identity and differences instead of the similarities that all people possessed - that they were wonderfully made by the same creator.

Bella continued to prattle on the entire ride to the pizza place, but while Cory tried to listen, his thoughts were occupied with the dinner ahead of them. On the surface, it was just pizza, but underneath it was so much more. This dinner could make or break Heidi's decision to help him out. He thought Bella was amazing, but he was also her father and more than a little biased.

"Yay, we're here," Bella hollered from the backseat. "Can I have a just cheese pizza, Daddy?"

"Sure, bug." He understood the appeal of just cheese for kids, but he was certainly glad this restaurant offered personal youth pizzas because he wanted some more ingredients on his pizza.

The small place was already filling up when Cory and

Bella entered, but Giada, the elderly female owner, still greeted them with a warm smile. "Cory, Bella, how are we tonight? Table for two?"

"Actually, we need a table for three tonight," Cory said, before she could lead them to their normal small table by the window.

"Three?" She glanced up as she pulled the menus out of the hostess stand. "You have someone joining you tonight?"

"We do," Cory said with a small smile. "An old friend."

"You didn't say she was old, Daddy."

"She?" Giada's eyes danced with delight. "In that case, I will set you up with the best seat in the house."

"That's really not necessary," Cory said, catching her innuendo. "She's just a friend from high school."

"I see," Giada said with a slight nod and an almost imperceptible wink. "Well, follow me, and I'll see what I can do."

Cory knew exactly what she was going to do. Not only was she going to sit them at her best table, but she probably had something special planned for the meal as well, and while he could continue to protest that nothing was going on, he couldn't help but wonder if a little extra might be just enough to convince Heidi this arrangement was worth it.

7

HEIDI

*H*eidi followed the directions of her GPS but was a little surprised to find herself in the parking lot of a small shopping center when it announced she had arrived at her destination. She scanned the storefronts for any indication that she was in the right place. Finally, near the far end, she spied a small fluorescent sign in the shape of a slice of pizza. That had to be the place.

The spicy aroma of garlic and tomato sauce greeted her as soon as she pulled open the glass door. Though small, the place was not lacking in charm. Her eyes scanned the beautiful murals of Italian country sides as she approached the hostess stand.

"Welcome to The Pizza Cafe. Is it just you tonight?"

The elderly woman's eyes slid to the space behind Heidi as if expecting someone else to appear.

"I'm meeting a friend. He should already be here. Cory Kingman?" Heidi scoured the room, but before she could say that she saw Cory, the woman was speaking again.

"You're Cory's friend. Oh, it's so nice to meet you. I'm Giada. I own this restaurant with my husband Luigi, and we just adore Cory and Bella. Follow me, dear."

Heidi followed the woman, curious as to the sudden shift in her demeanor. Cory had hinted he ate here often, but this woman acted like she knew him better than that.

"Here they are," Giada said, gesturing to Cory and a young girl who was drawing flowers and hearts all over the tablecloth, before turning back to Heidi with a sly smile on her face. She leaned in and whispered, "I'll let you two catch up." With that, she placed a menu on the table, flashed a wink at Heidi, and disappeared. What had Cory told her?

He was shaking his head as Heidi pulled out her chair and sat down. "I'm sorry about that. Giada gets to know her patrons, and when I mentioned I was meeting an old friend for dinner, she just assumed…" His voice trailed off, but the glance he shot towards his daughter told Heidi just what Giada had assumed. "Anyway, I'm glad you could make it. The food will not disappoint though I have to admit this will be my first time trying cashews on their pizza."

"You could have ordered something different for yourself."

"I could have," he said with a shrug of his shoulder, "but I figured why not join you? For old times' sake."

His eyes held hers for a moment, and Heidi felt that familiar spark. The same one she had felt all those years ago in high school. The one that warmed her insides and made her toes tingle. Did she still have feelings for him after all?

Cory shook his head slightly and turned his attention to his daughter. "Heidi, I'd like you to meet my daughter Bella. Bella, this is my friend Heidi."

The girl looked up from her drawings with wide brown eyes. Cory's eyes. "You don't look old. Daddy said you were an old friend."

Heidi smiled. Even to the children she taught, old was relative. Whenever one of them asked how old she was, she would let them guess. It never failed to amuse her when their guesses ranged from eighteen to over a hundred. "Well, sometimes old is relative. When your daddy said old, he didn't mean I was old in age but that we had known each other for a long time. We went to school together."

"Like when you were my age?"

Cory chuckled and Heidi's smile grew even wider. "Not quite that long ago. We met in high school."

Bella returned her focus to the tablecloth. "Daddy says I might go to your school this year."

Heidi's eyes shot to Cory. Had he already talked to Bella about the arrangement? She hadn't even agreed yet.

"I simply mentioned it was a possibility," he said with a shake of his head. "Nothing more." His emphasis on the last two words calmed her nerves slightly. He hadn't discussed the arrangement then. She didn't need to worry. Yet.

Giada returned at that moment with two pizzas and a Sprite for Heidi. She glanced to Cory who shrugged. "I took the liberty of ordering what used to be your favorite drink. If you don't like it, I'm sure Giada will get you something different."

"No, it's fine." Heidi just couldn't believe he remembered. Though she could tolerate a few flavors of dark cola now (those with cherry flavoring), she had hated all of them in high school and always insisted on ordering Sprites whenever she ate out. At home, she generally only drank tea or water, so carbonated beverages were like her treat to herself when she went out.

"I for one don't understand the appeal of nuts on pizza," Giada said, breaking into Heidi's memory, "but this one insisted." She nodded her head at Cory as she set the pizza down between them. "Said it was your favorite. Any man who will do that is a keeper in my book."

Heidi's cheeks heated up as Giada flashed her another wink before turning to Bella. "And here is a cheese pizza for the princess."

Bella giggled as she set her crayon aside. "I'm not a real princess, Ms. Giada."

"Well, you had me fooled." She smiled at Bella and then placed her hands on her hips as she surveyed the table. "Okay, you let me know if you need anything else. Enjoy!"

"Can I pray, Daddy?" Bella asked when Giada left.

"Of course. Go ahead."

Heidi bowed her head and closed her eyes as Bella began to speak.

"God is grace. God is good. Let us thank Him for this food. Amen."

Heidi bit back her smile. She was pretty sure there was more to that prayer, but it sounded so sweet coming from Bella's lips that she didn't want to say anything to make the girl feel bad. "Amen," she said.

"Amen," Cory echoed and grinned at Heidi. Probably just his way of thanking her for not embarrassing Bella.

Heidi grabbed a slice of pizza and shook a healthy dose of parmesan cheese on the top. Across the table, Cory snickered and shook his head. "What?"

"You. You haven't changed a bit. Still drowning the

taste of perfectly good pizza with that moldy cheese flavoring." He grabbed his own slice and placed it on his plate.

"It's not moldy, and it adds flavor. You've never given it a real chance."

"Uh, yes, I did. Do you not remember that time my Senior year when you convinced me to try it and I spent the rest of the night writhing on the bathroom floor?"

Heidi's eyes widened as the night he mentioned flew into her mind. "Okay, I do remember that, but it wasn't necessarily the cheese. It could have been something else."

A playful smile crossed Cory's lips. "Yeah, I suppose the crust or the toppings could have been moldy, except that no one else got sick."

"Hey, I had the same parmesan, and I didn't get sick," Heidi protested.

"Probably because you have a cast iron stomach from eating it all the time." He pointed a finger at her. "I'm pretty sure you're immune."

"What's immune mean?" Bella asked, joining the conversation after chewing her bite of pizza.

"Uh, it means you can't catch things like a cold or a runny nose," Heidi said, trying to explain the word in a way that Bella would understand.

"Oh, I wish I could be immune from skinned knees and tummy aches then," Bella said with a serious nod of her head. "I get those way too often."

Heidi bit the inside of her lip to keep from laughing aloud. "Yes, those would be good things to be immune from." Across the table, Cory smiled at her, and the three fell into a comfortable silence as they finished eating.

When everyone was sufficiently stuffed, the remaining food was boxed up, and the bill was paid, Heidi felt a small twinge of disappointment. This was the nicest dinner she'd had in a while. And definitely the least lonely.

"I don't want to rush you," Cory said softly as they walked toward the door, "but I do need to know if I should switch Bella's school as soon as possible. I would hate to start her in one place and then have to move her once school has started."

"Right. That would be hard." Heidi's mind still swirled with questions as she followed him to his car. Questions she couldn't very well ask with little ears listening. "I'd like to talk more about this, about how you see this going. Is there a time we could do that?"

Cory nodded and lifted Bella into the car. "Here you go, bug," he said, strapping her in and then handing her a travel white board and marker. "We'll get going in just a minute. I just need a minute to say goodbye to Ms. Heidi."

Bella nodded, but she was clearly already focused on her drawing. Cory shut her door and then turned once more to Heidi. "I get off early tomorrow and Bella can stay at the daycare until five. Will you have time before then?"

Heidi ran through her day in her head. She had a meeting in the morning and a few last-minute items to do in the classroom, but she could set aside some time in the afternoon. "I could meet up at three."

"Three is perfect. Do you still drink coffee?"

A soft heat spread across Heidi's cheeks. She'd been a coffee fiend in high school, and while she tried to limit herself to only one or two bought coffees a week, she still had at least one cup at home every day. "I do."

"Good, me too." His wide smile displayed his pearly white teeth and sent Heidi's heart thrumming a little faster in her chest. "There's a Coffee Bean close to your work. I assume you're familiar with it." His smile melded into a mischievous grin. "Meet me there at three tomorrow?"

"Sounds good." The words seemed innocent enough as they left her mouth, but were they? What was she going to tell him tomorrow? Was she going to agree to this arrangement? She had a night of long thinking and praying ahead of her.

They waved goodbye, and Heidi continued to her own car. Could she even consider this? Should she? Yes, she wanted a family and Bella seemed lovely, but what would happen when Cory left? Could she raise a child and work too? What if she did something wrong parenting Bella? Most people had the luxury of raising children from infants which gave them a few months of practice before the kid could cause havoc. Heidi would have nothing of the sort. No, if she agreed, she would be taking on an emotional five-year-old who had already been through the loss of her mother and would probably not take her father leaving lightly.

But...

Bella needed a home and security. And she'd already been uprooted so much. Was it fair to send her outside of the states? Plus, there was Cory, and while he might not love her, it was clear he did consider her a close friend. Marriages had been built on less. And become more.

"God, I could really use some advice on this," Heidi whispered as she looked up at the sky. Bright stars twinkled down from a dark sky, but no immediate sign flashed into her vision. However, she also knew God didn't always work that way. She would settle for a feeling of peace, but that didn't come immediately either.

"In His own time," she said softly and slid into the driver's side. She just hoped His time could match her timeline. At least a little.

8

CORY

"You in a hurry or something?" Tanner asked as Cory gathered up his things for the day.

"Yeah, sort of. I'm meeting Heidi again." He threw his jacket over his arm and scanned the desk one more time. He would not have time to come back if he forgot something.

"Again?" Tanner's voice lifted at the end, and his eyebrow arched on his forehead. "Did she agree to your proposal then?"

"I don't know," Cory said with a shake of his head. "She said she wanted to discuss some logistics, so I guess that means she's at least still considering it. We're meeting for coffee, so maybe I'll have an answer for you tomorrow."

Tanner chuckled. "I cannot believe this woman is even considering what you're asking. She must be a saint."

Tanner's words stopped Cory at the door. That's exactly what she was. Always had been. Even in high school, she'd tried to befriend kids who sat alone, volunteered to help with almost every project, and never complained about work - even the time they'd had to pull an all-nighter because he'd spilled coke on half of their evidence, making it unreadable. They'd had to reprint, relabel, and refile a ton of briefs and evidence. "Yeah, she is."

How had he forgotten how much he enjoyed Heidi's company? They'd been almost inseparable since his sophomore year when she'd joined the debate team and they'd been paired together. At first, he'd been annoyed. All the other sophomores had experienced upperclassmen as partners, and the rest of the incoming freshmen had been paired together. When he'd asked the teacher for an explanation, she'd said she saw something with the two of them that would work well together. And she'd been right. After a few bumpy first months, they had gone on to become the team in their district to beat.

When he left for college, he'd promised to keep in touch and come to as many of her tournaments as he could, but life and homework had gotten in the way, and he'd forgotten. Then he'd met Desiree, and she had consumed his focus.

"She definitely is," he repeated. "I'll let you know how it goes." With that, he flashed a wave over his shoulder and continued to his car.

Twenty minutes later, he pulled into the parking lot of the small coffee shop. Heidi was already sitting at a table in the back when he pulled open the glass door. He sent her a smile and a wave before motioning that he would join her after grabbing a coffee.

"What can I get for you suga'?" the woman behind the counter asked with a soft southern drawl.

"Americano with one pump of chocolate and cream please."

He forked over the three dollars for his coffee and then shuffled down to the end to wait for his name to be called. A moment later, steaming mug in hand, he slid into the chair across from Heidi.

"How was your day?" he asked as he blew into his drink. There was so much steam rising from it that he knew he would burn his tongue if he dared a sip right now.

"It was okay." Heidi stirred her frothy concoction with a straw. "Meetings this morning which always have the tendency to run long and be unnecessary for the most part."

Cory chuffed. He knew that all too well. The military was famous for calling meetings to discuss things that would go much faster in an email. Of course, looking at some of the young men who were joining now, he could see why the meetings were needed. More than once, he'd had to check up on a missing member only to find him holed up in his dorm room, playing video games. If he had a nickel for every time they claimed, they'd 'lost track of time,' he could retire and buy a house.

"But I did finish getting the room set up this afternoon, so it wasn't a total waste," she continued.

"How long does it take you to get set up every year?" Cory hadn't perused her room the other day when he'd been there, but he had noticed quite a few posters and other eye-catching materials adorning the walls.

"It depends on how much they make us take down at the end of the previous year. When they do a deep cleaning, we have to take everything off the walls. Those years, it takes me three whole days to get it all back up. The other years, I can leave the basic boards and I just have to change the inside pieces back to September's items - clocks, calendars, those types of things. I can usually finish in two afternoons if I'm lucky. And focused."

"Wow, I had no idea setting up a room took so much work."

Heidi chuckled. "Yeah, well, most people don't, but the kids notice. My first year, I hardly put anything up because I had nothing and I didn't know any better. The kids complained the whole first week about how boring my room was and how literally every other place they went was more interesting. I toured the rest of the classrooms that afternoon and they were right. Every room was colorful and engaging. Except mine. I swore never to be THAT teacher again."

"I can't imagine you ever being THAT teacher," Cory said with a laugh. "You were always so much fun in school. I'm sure the kids love you. In fact, I almost wish Bella were a year younger so she could have you as a teacher."

At those words, Heidi's smile slipped. "We should talk about Bella. She seems amazing, but I realized last night that I know nothing about her. How could I parent her? Why would she even trust me?"

Ah, yes, those were very good questions. Cory blew one more time into his cup as he thought about how best to answer. "Bella is amazing and trusting - sometimes a little too trusting. If I tell her she's safe with you, she'll believe me, and I'm pretty sure she likes you. She talked about you the whole way home last night, and while I can't promise she'll take my deployment well, she has been through one before as I mentioned yesterday. Unfortunately, we haven't really discussed them lately as I didn't think the Army would deploy me again with Desiree gone."

"Okay, but now that they are... what do you plan to tell her?"

Cory twisted his mug in small circles. "Well, I'd want

her to get to know you, spend time with you, but the time is short. Ideally, it would make the most sense to sit down and explain the marriage to her and have you move in. Then, you could see how we interact and she could get used to having you around."

Heidi stared into her drink for a moment as if mulling over his words. "Do you think we could pull off a wedding in less than thirty days?" she asked, looking up to meet his gaze.

"Wedding?" The word stuck in his throat like a large chunk of food. He knew he was proposing marriage, but to him it was merely a marriage of convenience. He hadn't actually thought of having another wedding, especially having already done that once.

"Well, yeah." The hesitation was clear in Heidi's halting words. "I mean I know you probably had one with Desiree, but I - if I agree to this - I haven't had one, and while I don't need anything big, I do have friends and family that would be quite sad if they didn't get to attend my wedding."

"Right." He should have thought of that. The wedding had been important to Desiree too, but he'd been young and in love then, so the massive amount of work it required had been worth it. He didn't want to go through that again, but he also didn't want to lose Heidi over a ceremony. If a ceremony was what she needed to agree to this, he would do it. Besides, Bella would probably love being in a wedding.

"I'll be honest, Heidi. I hadn't really thought about a wedding because, you're right, I have already had one, and this is more about Bella than myself."

All expression fell from Heidi's face, and she blinked. He knew that look. He'd only seen it once before - his Senior year when they'd missed advancing in state because the coach had gotten lost and they had missed their first round - but it was a look he would never forget. It was the one and only time he'd ever seen Heidi cry, and from the look on her face now he knew that tears would not be far behind.

"But," he continued, "I can also see why it would be important for you. I don't know what we can pull off in thirty days, but I can check with the chaplain. We could probably have a small ceremony at the chapel on base."

She pursed her lips and sniffed, but her expression was still unreadable as she held his gaze. "I prayed about this all last night," she finally said.

"And?" Cory's chest felt tight as he waited for her answer. Though he'd drifted away from God in the last year, he'd picked up on the fact that her faith was important to her. He should have known she would pray about the decision, but he didn't know what he would do if she said no.

Her gaze dropped to her straw, and she twirled it in

her cup as if brewing her next words with it. She was taking so long that Cory almost repeated his question. Instead, he pressed his lips together to keep them still. She'd heard; she was just... considering. She had always done this, always been the one to think carefully about what she was going to say. Except in debate tournaments. In those cases, she'd always seemed to have the right words, and they'd always flowed naturally. He had envied that about her.

"And... as much as I'm probably out of my mind, I can't bear the thought of that sweet little girl having her life thrown upside down again. If you think this is what's best for her-"

"I do," Cory jumped in, interrupting Heidi but unable to keep his mouth in check.

Heidi held up her hand. "And if we can have a small ceremony before you go, then I will agree to it."

Unable to stop himself, Cory jumped from his seat, grabbed Heidi's hand, and pulled her into a hug. "Thank you," he said, as he squeezed her tightly. "You have no idea what this means to me."

"I... you're welcome," Heidi said.

He pulled back at the stilted sound of her voice, but kept his hands on her shoulders. "No, really, Heidi. I owe you for this. Big time."

Her eyes held his, and for a moment, he thought he saw something flicker in them. Something like he'd seen in

Desiree's eyes when they'd first started dating. Something like... desire. But that couldn't be right. Heidi didn't feel that way about him, did she? They were just friends, right? Friends helping each other out.

"Well, we should probably hammer out the details," Heidi said, taking a step back and out of his reach.

As his hands returned to his sides, he tried to meet her gaze again - to dismiss his suspicion - but she did not meet his eyes. Instead, she slid back into her seat and resumed twirling her straw around. Still, she'd said yes, and he was probably reading more into her reaction than was really there.

"Yes, I suppose we should," he agreed, reclaiming his seat as well. "Where should we start?"

9

HEIDI

*H*eidi's heart was still thundering in her chest as Cory sat down across from her. She had known she still found Cory attractive, but she had not been prepared for the sensations that coursed through her body when he'd picked her up. It was like being on fire and freezing at the same time. The lingering heat from where his skin had touched hers still flickered.

"Um, I suppose we should start with the basics," she said, trying to focus on the issue at hand and not at the soulful brown of his eyes that threatened to draw her in and allow her to lose hours of time. "Like where will we live? You mentioned me moving in, but I have an apartment in town."

Oh geez, she hadn't even considered that until the words left her mouth. Would she have to pack up and move to his house or would they move into hers? And which thought scared her more?

Cory leaned back in the chair and ran a hand across his clean-shaven and very chiseled chin. "I hadn't thought about your apartment. I suppose it might be easier to move into your house since I'm sure it's closer to your work, and I won't need to be close to work for a while. On the other hand, Bella is already set up in our house which might or might not be a good thing. But there is added pressure being on base - crazy rules you have to follow. However, it is also safer."

The way Cory's sentences rambled one to the other told Heidi just how little he had thought this through. She supposed that had to do with the short notice, but she couldn't help wondering if this was really what he wanted or if he was making a snap decision that he would come to regret one day.

"Okay, two questions," Heidi said, placing a hand on Cory's arm to stop his rambling. "First, how big is your house?" Though she didn't really want to pack up and move, she lived in a small two-bedroom apartment. If his house was bigger, it only made sense for her to move.

Cory glanced down at her hand and then back up at her. Though she didn't want to remove it - she enjoyed the warmth of his skin beneath hers - she placed it back on her cup, allowing him to continue.

"It's about eighteen hundred square feet, I guess.

Three bedrooms, two baths. A small yard. The third bedroom is empty, so it would be easy to set you up there if that's the way we decide to go."

"Okay, second question. Does your house allow pets? I have a cat, and I'd really hate to give her up."

A soft smile curled Cory's lips. "Yes, we can have pets in the house."

"Okay, then it sounds like your house would be best. I only have a two bedroom, so there'd be no separate room for you, and mine is much smaller."

"Are you sure you're okay with that?"

Heidi was touched by the concern she not only heard in Cory's voice but saw in his eyes as well. He might not have thought this through completely, but it was clear that he understood how much more this would impact her than him. She thought about her apartment. It was home, but only because she'd decorated it the way she'd wanted and lived there for the last few years. However, it was small, and her neighbors next door often played their music too loud. Would she really miss it if she had to give it up?

"Would I be allowed to put a few of my touches on your house?" She hadn't seen his house, and maybe his tastes had changed since high school or maybe Desiree had decorated, but she could remember his room in high school being decorated with sports posters and trophies.

"If you mean like decor then of course, but there are

some things that the base won't allow us to do inside the houses simply because once we move out, they have to get it prepared for the next family quickly."

"Oh, like what?" Heidi realized she had no idea about base requirements. She would probably have to get a list of those so she didn't break them without knowing it.

"Um," Cory's brow furrowed. "There is something about interior paint though I think it's just that we have to repaint it white before we move, and I'm not sure we're allowed to change the flooring, but the only one I know of for sure is that we have to get approval for any home improvements from a committee. I honestly never looked into the others though I have heard there are more."

"You've never looked into them?" Heidi leaned forward across the table. "How do you know you aren't breaking them then?"

Cory shrugged. "Because I've never been talked to about any of them. Believe me, when you break a rule on base, you know about it. Heck, when you break a rule, nearly the whole neighborhood knows about it. It's kind of like a small town in that aspect."

"Oh, well that sounds nice, I think." Heidi had never lived in a small town, but she always enjoyed the charm of them when she watched them on movies. However, she also knew there were downsides, such as everyone knowing your business. Still, it might be a nice change considering she barely knew her neighbors at all, and the few she did, she had little in common with. Plus, Bella was sure to have some friends there. Maybe Heidi could meet a few of the other women as well. "So, how do we want to tell Bella? Do I just start coming over and hanging out with you guys?"

Cory's hand drifted to his chin once again. "Actually, since we'll have to have the ceremony soon, we should probably just sit her down and tell her. You could come over for movie nights and maybe a few hours on the weekends, so we could go to the park and I could show you the rest of the base. It will be a little annoying until we get married due to the ID checks at the front gate, but once we get married, you'll have your own ID card and will be able to come and go easier."

"Right, ID checks." Heidi hadn't even thought about that. It would be much harder for people to come visit her once she moved on base, but who honestly came to visit her now? Linley was about the only one, and she generally went over there instead. "What about church? Is Bella established somewhere? Because I really like my church and I sing on the worship team."

"Church," Cory blew the word out with a small sigh. "I haven't been great about church to be honest. Ever since Desiree died, I just haven't had the desire." His gaze shifted to the side as if she had touched on a sensitive topic.

Cory's behavior should have raised warning flags for

Heidi, but it didn't. She knew he had once been strong in his faith, and she knew that he was hurting now and would likely return to God when he was ready. "That's okay. It's understandable, but would you be okay with Bella coming with me?"

He shook his head. "No, that would be fine. She could probably use it."

"So, I'm sure I'll learn her bedtime routines and things over time, but you should think about how you want me to handle discipline. She seems like a great kid, but I'm sure there will be things that crop up with you leaving. I'd like to know how you handle them so I can be on the same page."

Cory blinked at her as if the thought had never occurred to him. "Yeah," he ran his hand across his chin again, "yeah, I'll have to think about that. I guess there's a lot I didn't really think through."

"Are you sure you still want to do this?" Heidi asked.

His hand fell from his face and reached across the table to grab hers. "I don't have a choice, Heidi. I would be lying if I said it doesn't scare me, but leaving her with you scares me much less than leaving her with anyone else."

It wasn't the answer she had expected to hear, and it certainly wasn't romantic, but Heidi could understand his position. She couldn't imagine how she would feel if she was forced to leave a child, but she believed she would want to leave the child with a friend if a relative wasn't possible.

"Then we will find a way to make this work, Cory. I promise."

He held her gaze a moment longer before squeezing her hand one last time. "Thank you for agreeing to this. So, would you like to start tonight?"

"Tonight sounds good," Heidi said. "Shall I bring something to make for dinner?"

Relief flooded Cory's features. "That would be amazing. Besides the pizza last night, Bella and I have been living off Mac N Cheese and Peanut Butter and Jelly sandwiches."

Heidi chuckled as she shook her head, but she was not surprised. Cory had shown no desire to cook in high school, and she doubted he'd had much need after with the military first providing his meals and then his wife. "Okay, I'll bring ingredients for a simple chicken dish. Maybe Bella would like to help?"

A small smile crossed Cory's perfect lips. "I bet she would. She used to love to watch Desiree cook..." his smile faltered, and his gaze fell to the table, "before she got sick."

Heidi's heart went out to him. She'd been wallowing in self-pity lately, but he had gone through so much more than she had. "Hey, it will be okay," she said, placing her hand on his arm.

His hand fell over hers, and he squeezed. "It will be now. Thanks to you."

Heidi tried not to think about the heat that had traveled up her arm every time they touched as they finished their coffees and said goodbye. She needed to continue telling herself that this was not a relationship. It was an agreement between friends and nothing more, but saying it didn't make it any easier to believe.

As she pulled out of the parking lot, she thought of everything she needed to do. The list was long, but two things rose to the top. She needed to call Linley and she needed to go see her parents. The latter could wait for the weekend when she had time to drive up to their place and come up with the best way to tell them, but Linley needed to know now. After all, if she was going to try and plan a wedding in fewer than thirty days, she was going to need some help.

Heidi pulled over to make the call, but as her fingers pressed the buttons, doubt rose in her mind. She hadn't been lying when she'd told Cory she'd prayed about it the previous night, and she did feel that God was nudging her in this direction. But, now that the wheels were in motion, worry was rearing its ugly head.

What if she'd misread the feelings? What if what she thought was God nudging her was really just her fear of ending up alone taking over? What if she was a terrible mother and messed up his daughter for life? Suddenly, her chest felt like it was being suffocated by a hundred-pound weight. Heidi placed her hand over her heart and tried to calm her breathing. When it was under control, she finished dialing Linley's number and hit send.

"Tell me I'm not crazy," she said when Linley answered.

"I can't do that since I'm pretty sure you are," Linley said with a laugh. "It's one of the things I love about you. What have you supposedly done that is so crazy?"

"I agreed to Cory's marriage proposal." The words sounded so crazy as they left her mouth that she uttered them as quickly as possible, hoping that would help. It didn't.

"Okay, you're right. For most people that would be crazy, but I know you Heidi, and I know you didn't enter into this decision lightly. Let me guess, you were up late last night praying about it?"

"Yes, and I thought last night that I was at peace with the decision, but now I'm no longer sure. What if I mess everything up?" Heidi ran a hand across her forehead and down her cheek in frustration.

"Is that what you're really afraid of?" Linley asked.

"Yes." Heidi spat the word out but then paused. *Was* that what she was really afraid of? "No, I don't know."

"I think you're more afraid that he won't love you back." Linley's voice was sage and serious.

"What? I don't even love him. Why would I worry he

wouldn't love me back?" Even as she protested, the words held a ring of truth for Heidi. She wasn't sure she loved Cory, but she had once, and she could easily see herself falling for him again, but what if he never returned her feelings? Could she live with that?

"Because you are a romantic, Heidi. You have talked of true love since the day I met you. You record every Hallmark Christmas movie that airs and watch them well into July. I think what you are doing is extremely noble, but I worry how you will feel if this marriage is always just friendship."

Heidi pursed her lips and drummed her fingers on the steering wheel. Linley was right, but Heidi also felt that she was right - that stepping up was the right thing to do. She supposed it boiled down to trust. She needed to step back and trust that God was in control. It was definitely harder to do than to say, but she'd been trying to work on it for the last few years.

"It will all work out," Heidi said. "It has to, and I'm not doing it for me. I'm doing it for him and for his daughter." She paused and took a deep breath. "Anyway, Cory agreed to a small wedding, but we don't have much time. Tell me you'll help me plan it."

"Of course I will, but how much time is not much time?"

Heidi chewed on the corner of her bottom lip. "Fewer than thirty days."

"Thirty days?" Even though Heidi couldn't see Linley in person, she could picture her gaping mouth and incredulous expression.

"It's doable, right? If we keep it small and simple." Heidi nibbled again on the corner of her bottom lip. It had to be doable. It was the one thing she had asked for in the arrangement.

"It might be tough, but you know me. I love a challenge."

Heidi could tell that Linley was forcing her chipper tone, but she appreciated it all the same. "That's true and what better time to challenge ourselves than right at the beginning of a new school year, right?"

She shook her head as the words cemented in her mind. This really was the worst time to throw her life into chaos. What on earth had she been thinking?

10

CORY

"What are we having for dinner tonight, Daddy?" Bella asked as she padded into the kitchen.

Cory looked up from the document he was working on. "Actually, my friend Heidi from last night is coming over tonight, and she's going to make some dinner. Would you like to help her?"

Bella's eyes lit up as her head bobbed up and down. "Yes, please. I want to learn to cook. No offense, Daddy, but sandwiches get boring sometimes."

Cory chuckled as he shut the laptop and stood to put it away. It was almost six and the front gate office should be calling at any moment to verify Heidi's purpose on base. "I know they do, bug, but my friend will be spending a lot more time with us. I bet we'll get to eat a lot of meals that are better than sandwiches. Maybe we'll even learn how to make them."

Bella's brow furrowed. "If she's going to be spending more time with us, does that mean she's your girlfriend?"

Though he had known this question would be coming, it still caught him off guard. Instead of answering right away, he decided to see how she would feel. "Would that be bad if she was? I know your mother hasn't been gone very long, so you can be honest with me."

Her lips pursed as she thought. "I miss Mommy, but I also miss having a mommy around, and I think you do too. Besides, Ms. Heidi seemed nice. I'm okay with it if you want her to keep coming over and hanging out with us."

While he didn't need his daughter's permission, her words did make him feel a little better about dragging Heidi into their lives. "Okay, well let's get the house prepared for her then, huh? Can you make sure all the clothes are picked up in the living room?"

He had a habit of leaving clothes on the floor of his bathroom when he removed them at the end of the day, but Bella was notorious for leaving a trail of clothes wherever she went. She was like a little tornado without the destruction. Shoes would end up by the couch or under the kitchen table depending on when she removed them, socks were almost always in the living room though never near each other, and the rest of her clothes usually formed a trail down the hallway to the bathroom.

"Okay, and then I'll pick the stuffies I want to show her the most."

Cory shook his head as Bella skipped off. That girl had more stuffed animals than she knew what to do with, but many of them had been sent when Desiree died, and he didn't have the heart to get rid of them. He had, however, made himself a promise not to buy her any more no matter how hard she begged.

As his gaze swept the kitchen to see if it needed tidying, his phone rang. The front gate. "Hello," he said after punching the button on his cell.

"Sergeant Kingman? This is Specialist Hill at the front gate. There is a Heidi Brighton here who says she is expected. Can you verify please?"

"Yes, in fact, is it possible to get her a thirty-day visitor's pass? She'll be coming over often in the next month."

"Yes, sir. Thank you."

The thirty-day pass would allow her entrance to the base without having to stop and call, but they were only offered once, which was fine in his case since they would be married before this one expired.

Knowing that she was now only about five minutes out, he wiped off the counter and table for good measure. Then his eyes scanned the rest of the area. It was more cluttered than he would have liked, but Desiree had always been the order keeper of the house. He'd tried his best after she was gone, but Bella was like a storm and wherever she went, a mess invariably followed. Cleaning up after her was a full-time job. He wondered if Heidi was still as much of a neatnik as she'd been in high school.

Before he had time to ponder that thought any longer, the doorbell rang.

"She's here," Bella called as she came racing toward the door like a Tasmanian Devil, a stuffed animal tucked under each arm. "I can't wait to show her all my stuffies."

Cory chuckled and shook his head as he unlocked the front door. He knew she taught preschoolers, but he hoped she enjoyed being bombarded with attention even after work.

"Hi," she said, flashing a timid smile as she held up two large bags filled with supplies. "I guess I'm in the right place?"

"You are indeed." He stepped back and ushered her inside. "Did you have any trouble finding it?"

Before Heidi had a chance to answer, Bella interrupted, holding up her stuffies for examination. "Ms. Heidi, I brought out my favorite stuffed animals to show you, but I have a lot more in my room. I want you to see all of them."

Heidi's lips parted in a wide smile as she bent down to

be more on Bella's level. "Who do we have here? A bunny and a lamb?"

Bella nodded. "This is Bunny," she said, pulling the now slightly grayish creature closer to her face. "I got her when I was born, but then I lost her for a time." She leaned closer as if sharing a secret. "I put her in one of my mom's old purses and forgot she was there. I was so sad that Mimi sent me this lamb to cheer me up." She leaned back and shoved the only slightly less gray lamb in Heidi's face. "Later, I found Bunny, so now I have both." Her mouth twisted to one side. "I don't know who I love more though."

Heidi's tone was serious and friendly as she answered Bella. "You know, I think that's okay. It's perfectly fine to love both of them the same."

Cory marveled at how good she was with Bella. He knew that probably came with the territory - her being a teacher and all - but he'd also known many adults who couldn't interact with kids the way she did.

"If you can give me just a second to talk to your dad and set these bags down, I'll come see all your stuffed animals, and you can tell me all of their names before I make us dinner."

"Okay," Bella said with a smile. "I'll go get them ready." She spun and scampered off down the hallway back to her room.

"That was amazing," Cory said as he watched his

daughter leave. "I can never get her to give me a few minutes when she is wound up like that."

"Well, the secret is that you have to let her get her say out first," Heidi said, standing back up. "I've learned that, especially with young kids, their brains can only do one thing at a time well. So, if you want their attention, let them talk first and then they are more willing to do what you need them to do."

"That actually makes a lot of sense." Cory had never thought about the fact that Bella might not be able to focus on what he was asking her to do because she was so focused on what she felt like she needed to say.

"It's the saving grace of a preschool teacher. The first year, I was so exhausted because I spent most of the day trying to refocus them and never feeling like I got anything done. When I began incorporating a sharing time, and they knew they would get to say what was on their minds, it got so much better." She lifted the bags still hanging from her hands. "So, want to show me the kitchen?"

"Of course, I'm so sorry. Let me take those for you." Chagrin and a soft heat flooded Cory's cheeks as he took the bags from her. He couldn't believe he'd left her holding them for so long. "In fact, if you aren't starving, how about we set these down, and I give you the tour? Don't worry, it's short."

"I'd like that," Heidi said.

As Cory showed her into the kitchen, he tried to see it

from her eyes. The walls were a stark white as they had never bothered to request the ability to repaint them. Any home alterations needed approval, and since they would have had to paint the walls white before they moved out and they hadn't planned on staying long, they hadn't even bothered to inquire about it, but Desiree had tried to bring some warmth into the room with accents. A big fan of Italy, she'd hung several pictures of Italian bistros and landscapes. The towels and pot holders continued the theme with their soft purple and tan colors. But it certainly wasn't a high-end kitchen. The countertops were a plain white Formica and not the marble most houses used, and the floors were gray cement - great for cleaning but not aesthetically appealing. They were also very cold in the winter.

"As you can see, it isn't much, but there is a small pantry and there's room to prepare dishes - not that Mac N Cheese takes up much space," he said with a slight chuckle.

"Well, the white is a little jarring, but I love the colors in the decor. I'm a big fan of Italy," Heidi said as her eyes continued to scan the small area.

Cory set the bags on the counter and pointed toward the small nook that served as the dining room. "This is the dining room. Not fancy, but big enough for us." The table was small, only big enough for four, but he had few occasions to need anything bigger.

"It's homey," Heidi said, but the way she said it made him wonder if she really meant it.

"It's home for now, anyway. We had always planned to move off base one day and get a nicer house, but we took the house when we first got here so that we wouldn't have to rush into any purchase decision. Then, Desiree got sick and buying a house just fell to the side. And after," he shrugged. After, he'd had no desire to look for another place. There were definitely times he thought about it, times when something in the house would trigger a memory of Desiree, but looking required energy, and all of his currently went to work and then taking care of Bella.

Heidi stepped to him and placed a hand on his arm. Her voice was warm and soft as she spoke, like a soothing balm on a hot sunburn. "You don't have to sell me on the place, Cory. I live in a small two-bedroom apartment. My neighbors play Metallica until midnight every night, and I can hear it, and everything else, through the walls. The place might be newer and have more carpeting, but at least you have some quiet here."

He glanced down at her hand. It was a simple touch, but for some reason it was sending pulses of heat up his arm. Pulses he didn't understand. "Yeah, we definitely have quiet." He looked up from his arms and caught her gaze. Her blue eyes were like a serene sea at sunset -

warm, inviting - the kind of eyes he could get used to staring into.

Blinking, he cleared his throat and stepped away from her, breaking the connection that he didn't know how to process at the moment. "Here, let me show you the rest." What was going on with him? He'd spent time with her like this in the past, but he'd never felt emotions like he was feeling now.

He turned toward the hallway, both to continue the tour and to conceal his confusion. As she'd already seen the living room when she entered, the only thing left was the bathrooms and bedrooms.

"This is the guest room which you can decorate any way you'd like," he said as he opened the door to the room that Desiree had planned to turn into a home office. It held only an empty desk and a chair as she'd gotten sick before they'd been able to set it up. "I assume you'll have furniture, so I can remove these pieces if you need."

"I do have furniture," Heidi said, "though your living room seems well-stocked. I may have to find a new home for my stuff or at least an inexpensive storage unit."

"I think we have access to a storage unit here on base if needed." He'd never had the need to look into one, but he'd heard some of the younger guys talk about it as they generally lived in the barracks that were already furnished.

"That should be fine, and my furniture was all hand-me-downs from my parents anyway, so it's not a big deal if

I just need to pass it on to someone else." She smiled up at him. "Hard to afford the newest stuff on a teacher's salary, especially with the rent here in Washington."

Cory nodded. He didn't know what teachers made, but he knew what he made, and it couldn't be much more. "Well, one good thing is that my check pays for the house here, so you can save on rent for the foreseeable future."

Her eyes twinkled as she nibbled softly on her bottom lip. "Yeah, I guess I can."

Her lips? Why was he focusing on her lips? His heart did another funny little dance in his chest as she held his gaze, and he forced himself to look away and focus on the tour. "Right, well, across the hall is the bathroom. It's small, and this room shares it with Bella, but you are welcome to use mine whenever you need as well, though it's not much bigger."

He flipped the light on in the small bathroom and cringed at the green smears of toothpaste streaking the sink. Cleaning the bathroom had slipped his mind the last few days, and while he was glad Bella was brushing her teeth, it appeared she needed another reminder of how much toothpaste to use and how to wash away the excess.

"I take it you don't use this one often." The teasing humor was evident in Heidi's voice, and he didn't need to look at her to know she was biting back a grin.

"No, but I'll have another talk with Bella about cleaning up after herself."

"Are you ready to see my room now, Ms. Heidi?" Bella asked, poking her head out of her room as if she'd heard their voices and been patiently waiting for a pause in the conversation.

Heidi looked to Cory as if passing the question on to him. "All that's left is the master bedroom and bath, which can wait for another time if you want." Actually, he'd be slightly relieved if she did want to wait. The thought of her in his bedroom and bathroom didn't bother him per se, but it did stir up something inside that he wasn't sure he was ready to tackle yet.

"Okay, then it shall wait, and I shall see what Bella has to show me." Heidi flashed him a smile before taking Bella's outstretched hand and following her into the room.

As Cory watched them disappear, he tried to make sense of the conflicting emotions he was feeling. Heidi was just a friend, and this marriage was only to help him out, so why did he feel like he was betraying Desiree and what were these tingles and weird feelings he kept getting all about?

11

HEIDI

"Now what?" Bella asked as Heidi put the finishing touches on the dinner.

"Now we set the table. Do you think you can do that?"

Bella beamed and puffed out her little chest. "I can definitely set the table. It's my job every night, so I'm really good at it."

"I bet you are," Heidi said with a smile before grinning at Cory. He had been watching them as she made dinner and let Bella help. Now, he stared at her with an expression she couldn't quite place. In fact, from the faraway look in his eyes, she was no longer sure he was looking at her as much as watching something only he could see. "Can you get some drinks?" she asked him.

"What?" He blinked at her and shook his head. "Oh, right, of course."

As he opened a cabinet and pulled out cups, Heidi wished she could read minds. She was definitely curious what he was thinking. It had been obvious from his behavior during the tour that she was affecting him. What she didn't know was whether she was affecting him in a good way or a bad one.

With the table set, the trio sat down and enjoyed the dinner Heidi had prepared. When it was over, Bella helped clear the table before disappearing back to her room.

"So, what do you normally do after dinner?" Heidi asked Cory as he put on a pot of coffee.

"Honestly?" He folded his arms across his chest and leaned against the counter. "This is my one quiet hour before it's time to get Bella ready for bed, so usually I catch up on emails or watch the news."

The corners of Heidi's lips twitched. That was usually what she did about this time of night as well. "I don't want to interrupt your routine, but do you think you could skip tonight, so we could hammer out some more details?"

"Sure," Cory said, turning his attention back to the coffee pot as it began to fill. "What did you have in mind?"

"Well, I guess the first thing is to set a date for the wedding. I know you said your deployment was in fewer than thirty days, but I'm not exactly sure how much time that gives me if there are other things that have to be done after the wedding."

"Right." Cory pulled down two mugs and held one up for Heidi in question. She nodded and waited for him to continue. "There definitely are some things we would need to do, like getting you an ID card and setting up the will and power of attorney. They usually don't take that long as long as there are openings, but two weeks would probably be plenty of time. My deployment date is set for October first, so the wedding should be no later than mid-September, I think. Maybe we could push it out to the 20th."

Mid-September? That was only a little over two weeks away. Thirty days hadn't seemed like much, but it certainly did now. Two weeks left her almost no time, especially with the start of school, and the thought of pulling together a wedding so quickly certainly put her stomach in knots, but not as much as the words "power of attorney" and "will." She hadn't really thought about what would happen if Cory didn't come back.

"That fast? Okay. Were you able to speak to the chaplain today?"

"I was. He has an opening September 15th and 16th and then one on the 21st though that would be pushing it."

Heidi pulled out her phone and tapped on her calendar app. The fifteenth was a Saturday which made the most sense, especially if they had it in the late afternoon or early evening. Sunday wasn't a bad option either, but she didn't want it to interfere with church.

"The fifteenth it is then." She had no idea what she would be able to pull off that quickly, but suddenly it seemed a lot less important. The thought of Cory not returning had firmly taken root in her mind, and she switched back to that topic. "We should discuss what that would look like as well," she said as he handed her a mug and a bottle of creamer.

He took the seat across from her and blew on his mug. "What?"

"The will." Heidi dropped her eyes to her mug, finding the words hard to say. "I hadn't really thought about anything happening to you. I'm assuming you would want her grandparents to take her if something did."

"Oh," his eyes dropped to his mug as if this conversation was as uncomfortable for him as it was for her, "yeah, wills become a part of military life pretty quickly. My job is actually pretty safe, but they don't like any surprises. As for Bella, I guess she would have to go to Italy to live with my parents. Although they are getting older. Maybe we should talk about that topic more as the date gets closer?" His eyes flicked to hers and held the same question.

"Sure, we can do that." Heidi added a little creamer and stirred her coffee. She would just have to force the thought from her mind for now. "Okay, so I know you already had a ceremony, but do you want to be involved in the planning of this one? Is there anything you really want or really don't want?" She lifted her gaze to meet his again.

His lips folded in as a line sprouted across his forehead. "I don't mind helping you plan it, but I'm not particular. The only thing I can't do is German chocolate cake." He shook his head.

"The coconut flakes," they said at the same time.

Heidi laughed. He might have changed a little since high school, but some things were definitely still the same. "Okay, no German chocolate cake. I was thinking light pink and baby blue for the colors. Any objections?"

"Can we go with a slightly darker blue?" he asked as his face wrinkled in disgust. "Baby blue always reminds me of either babies or those horrible suits from the seventies."

Laughter spilled from Heidi's lips. "Okay, the seventies suits I understand, but what's wrong with babies?"

"Nothing, but I'd rather not look like one at my wedding."

Suddenly the image of Cory dressed in a pale blue onesie invaded her mind, and she pressed her hand over her mouth to keep from spewing the coffee she had just taken a sip of.

Cory's eyes widened in alarm. "Are you okay?"

Heidi held up a finger and nodded as she attempted to swallow without choking. "I am. I just had this image of you as a baby." She shook her head, unable to keep the smile from gracing her lips. "It was not a pretty picture."

"Hey, I'll have you know I was a very cute baby," Cory said, feigning a hurt expression.

"I'm sure you were when you were little, but as a grown man? Not so much."

His nose wrinkled in disgust. "Yeah, I suppose not. Why would you picture that anyway?"

Heidi reached across the table and swatted his arm. "You're the one who brought it up."

He glanced down at her hand and then back up at her. "I guess I did. So, can we agree? No baby blue."

"Yes, we can agree. Actually, since it will be fall, perhaps a darker blue and a magenta or purple would be more fitting anyway." Her hand was still on his arm, and his eyes were still on her, sending her heart skipping in her chest.

"Those colors sound perfect," he said, holding her gaze.

Heidi's breath caught as they stared at each other. Something was definitely happening between them.

"Daddy, I'm getting tired," Bella's voice broke the moment, and a minute later, she appeared in the kitchen, rubbing her eyes with one hand while the other clutched her stuffed animal tightly.

Disappointment flooded Heidi as Cory turned to his daughter. She wasn't mad at the girl, but she wished her timing was a little better. The need to know what might have happened between them burned inside her. "I should get going anyway." She removed her hand but immediately missed the warmth.

"Right, I'm sure you have things to do to finish preparing for school. Speaking of which, will anyone be in the office tomorrow who can help me with paperwork for Bella?"

"Of course, our office staff will be there until four."

"Great, I'll stop in to see you when I drop by. Maybe we can finish this conversation. I can take a long lunch break if you want to check a few places out."

"Yeah, I'll make some calls in the morning." Heidi assumed he was talking about picking out the cake, but she already knew of the bakery she wanted a cake from. She just needed to make sure they could deliver on such short notice. However, he could have been talking about the wedding attire, and that, on the other hand, was another matter. She would have to spend some time this weekend shopping for a dress, in case alterations would be needed.

"Thanks for showing me how to cook, Ms. Heidi. Can we do it again?"

Heidi smiled and pulled Bella in for a hug. "That we can, Miss Bella. I'll see you again soon."

"Yay."

She managed to get the word out before a giant yawn

took over. Heidi had worked with kids long enough to know that a total pass out wasn't far behind.

"I'll see you tomorrow," she said to Cory as she stood and headed toward the front door.

"Tomorrow." It was only one word, but somehow it felt like it held the promise of so much more.

CORY

"Wow, I did not realize how much paperwork there was for a Kindergartner," Cory said as he entered Heidi's classroom. The stack of papers in his hand was really only about five sheets stapled together, but it felt a lot thicker.

Heidi looked up from her desk with a smile. "Yeah, it's a process, but I think you only have to do it once."

"Thank goodness. I'll probably have writer's cramp when I'm done with all of this. So, we discussed colors last night, but did you have other thoughts you wanted to hash out? I know I said it doesn't really matter to me, but I don't want you to have to do all the planning yourself."

In actuality, he'd thought he didn't want another wedding ceremony - and he definitely didn't want one as big and arduous as his first - but he had to admit he'd had fun discussing one with Heidi, and he knew that due to the time limits, and her personality, that it would be a smaller affair.

Her eyes twinkled, and her grin widened. "Actually, yes. I thought today we could check out this bakery I love and see if they can do the cake."

A feeling of relief filled him. He would have gone tux shopping with her, but he found the chore of buying clothes boring as it was. Food, however, was right up his alley. "Sounds good." He checked his watch to verify his time. "I have another hour before I have to be back at work. Will that be enough time?"

"That should be perfect. Let me get my purse, and we can go." She grabbed her bag and led the way out of her classroom.

Twenty minutes later, they were seated at a small table in a cozy establishment called The Backdoor Bakery. The woman, a young eclectic millennial complete with purple hair and a nose ring, had handed them a menu of all the types of cakes they made along with prices and promised to bring out the sample tray shortly.

"What's with the name?" Cory asked as he took in the interior. The place had a chic warehouse vibe with leather couches and vintage chairs underneath exposed beams and metal pipes. A small fire crackled from the center fireplace. Every table in the place was different, giving it a garage sale feel but not in a bad way.

Heidi smiled. "The woman who owns this bakery had very little money when she first started. She baked in her own kitchen and sold her cakes from her back door until she raised enough to buy a small shop. This was originally only one shop, but she was able to work hard enough to buy the one next door when it went up for sale and tear down the wall."

She pointed to a small line that ran the length of the floor. "If you look closely, you can see where that wall used to be."

"That's quite an inspiring story," Cory said.

"It is and it's just another reason that I love this place." The nose-ringed woman arrived then with a large platter filled with bite sized pieces of cake in all colors. Heidi smiled up at her. "Thank you."

The woman nodded and scurried off to help another customer.

Heidi turned her attention back to Cory. "After you try these, you'll understand the other reason."

Cory scanned the offerings. They all looked good, and he had no idea how to choose a starting point. "Okay, where do I start?"

"How about we just start at one end and work our way to the other?"

Cory nodded and one by one, they tried each of the tiny morsels of goodness. Heidi had not been wrong. All of them were delicious, and at the end, Cory not only felt completely stuffed, but they had only narrowed it down to four choices.

"The way I see it is that we can order two cakes. There's usually the main one and then the groom's cake, so we really only have to eliminate two choices. Out of the final four, which was your least favorite?"

Cory stroked a hand across his chin as he regarded the list again. "I guess I'd have to say the chocolate with raspberry filling. It just didn't have the same pizzazz as the others."

"Pizzazz?" Heidi asked with a smile. "We're talking about cake here, not some new outfit."

"You know what I mean," Cory said, narrowing his gaze at her.

"I do. Okay, I think I'll eliminate," her face scrunched up as she thought, "the vanilla cake with the fudge middle."

"Well, then I think we've made our choice," Cory said.

"I guess we have." Heidi's lips tilted up at the ends, and something twisted in Cory's stomach.

He really needed to stop focusing on her lips or he was going to find himself wanting to kiss them. His watch buzzed against his wrist, alerting him that he needed to get his butt back to work. "All right then," he said, grateful for the distraction, "I should get back to work, but can I help with the ordering process?" Every bone in his body was telling him that he needed to escape, clear his head, but leaving her to finish the order alone also felt wrong.

"No, go ahead," Heidi said. "I'll get the order set up. I need to go see my parents this weekend and soften the blow of this rushed wedding, but should we tell Bella next week?"

"Bella, yes, we can do that." Cory stood and pushed his chair in as if making it a barrier between himself and Heidi which felt silly because Heidi was just his friend, right? His friend whose lips kept appearing in his mind. "Do you want me to come with you to tell your parents?" He extended the offer because it was the right thing to do, but his gut clenched at the thought of facing her parents.

"Aw, that's sweet of you to offer, but I think I should tell them myself." Her lips pulled in together, and a tiny worry line creased her forehead. "I'm not exactly sure what their reaction will be."

"Right. Should I get you a ring? Would that help?" He felt like slapping his forehead. He should have already gotten her a ring. His proposal had been bad enough. The least he could do was get her a nice ring.

Heidi blinked at him. "I hadn't even thought about a ring. It's really not necessary since this is really only a marriage on paper, right?"

Was that a note of hope in her voice? That maybe this was something more? Did he want it to be something more? His gut clenched again. "Yeah, I guess you're right. Though I will get you one for the ceremony."

The light faded from her eyes. "Of course, the ceremony."

Cory hated the hurt look in her eyes, hated that he was the one making her feel this way. A part of him wanted to reach out and brush her cheek, to tell her everything would be okay, but he honestly wasn't sure of that. At least not at the moment. All he felt at this moment was confusion. Head spinning, gut aching confusion, and as much as he wanted to reassure her, he needed to figure out his own feelings first. She would be even more hurt if he said something in the heat of this moment that he wouldn't be able to back up later.

"Well, anyway, thanks again for this. It was fun." Fun? He felt like a coward. Why couldn't he just tell her how he felt? Surely, she would understand his confusion. She was probably feeling something like it as well.

She stood and offered a smile. "You're welcome. Talk soon?"

"Yes. Soon." With that, he flicked his hand in an awkward wave before turning and heading to his car.

Cory was still sorting through his renegade thoughts when he walked back into his office ten minutes later.

"Whoa, what's with the face?" Tanner asked.

Cory shook his head, trying to put his finger on what it

was exactly that was bothering him. "I just did a cake tasting with Heidi."

"Okay, but you like cake, so what's the problem?"

"It was a cake testing for the upcoming wedding," Cory said as if that explained everything.

"And?" Tanner lifted his shoulder with a shrug. "You do remember cakes being a part of weddings, right? I mean I know it's been a while, but I didn't think your memory was that bad."

Cory scratched at his chin. "No, of course I remember that. It's just that this wedding wasn't supposed to mean anything. It was simply the means to an end, you know?"

Tanner tilted his head, a line of confusion creasing his face. "Are you saying that now it does?"

"I don't know," Cory said, sinking onto the edge of the desk. "She's always just been Heidi before - my good friend and debate partner - but now she's in my house and making my daughter smile and making me feel things I haven't felt in a long time."

"And that's bad?" Tanner's brow lifted even higher.

"Yes, that's bad. I'm not supposed to be having feelings for her. I'm not supposed to be having feelings for anybody. This is a marriage of convenience, remember?"

Tanner held up his hands in a defensive gesture. "Hey, don't yell at me. I'm just trying to figure out why it's a big deal, and maybe it's not what you think. It has been a while since you've had a woman around. Maybe it's just that."

"Yeah," Cory latched onto that idea. "Yeah, you're right. I'm sure it's just that. That and seeing her again after so long." Maybe if he said it enough times, he could convince himself.

"Yeah, I'm sure that's all it is," Tanner said, but his smirk said otherwise.

Cory shook his head as he turned on his computer. Even if that wasn't all it was, it would have to be. There was no way he was ready for a real relationship or even opening his heart again. Was he?

13

HEIDI

*H*eidi inhaled deeply as she stared at the quaint house in front of her. It had never been a large or elaborate house as her parents tended to sink more money into the vineyard itself than the house that sat at the front of the property, but it had always been home. A place of comfort and love and never a place of fear. Until now.

Maybe fear wasn't quite the right word. She was a grown woman after all, and it wasn't like her parents were going to punish her. She didn't even need their approval. But she wanted it. Her family had always been close, and as right as she felt this marriage of convenience was, she wanted her parents to accept it. To accept Cory.

"Please Lord, help them understand," she whispered as she withdrew her key and stepped from her car.

The front door opened before she reached the porch, and her mother came running out, the essence of joy and sunlight filling her smile.

"Heidi, it's so good to see you."

"You too, Mom," Heidi said as she wrapped her arms around her mother. The two were nearly the same height - often confused for sisters instead of mother and daughter due to her mother's youthful appearance - a trait that Heidi hoped had been passed on to her.

"I'm so glad you found time to come out here before school started," her mother said as she led Heidi into the house. "Your father has been working on a new wine, and I know he would love to get your opinion on it."

"Of course. I'd be happy to sample," Heidi said, hoping her smile appeared genuine and not as forced as it felt on her face at the moment. She wanted to enjoy the time with her parents, especially since her schedule made it harder to get out to see them more often, but the weight of her impending announcement hung about her, like a necklace made of plutonium.

"So, tell me all about the new school year. Are you ready? Have you met any of your kids yet?"

Heidi loved that her mother was so involved in her career, even if she didn't necessarily understand all the nuances of teaching. Though she sometimes got a list of names of her students a few days before school started, she almost never met them until the day before, and that was only if they attended the offered "meet the teacher" day. Otherwise, she met them the first day of school.

"Well, the classroom is in order. I haven't met any of them yet, but I'm sure it will be just as good as last year. The kids are always the highlight of my year."

At least that part was true. Though there were always a few challenging students, Heidi loved working with preschoolers. Their pure delight in learning and innocence in everything else gave her faith that humanity was not entirely doomed.

"That's good," her mother said as they reached the kitchen. Evidently, she had been in the process of making lunch when Heidi arrived because her mother grabbed a tray of something and popped it in the oven before turning back to Heidi. "And how is the dating front going?"

"Well, that's actually why I'm here," Heidi said as she took a seat on one of the barstools. The wooden chair was not decorative or especially comfortable, and she shifted in the seat, trying to find a spot that felt right. It was impossible, but Heidi knew most of that stemmed from her nervousness and not the chair itself.

"Oh?" Her mother's eyes widened with an impish glow. "What's his name and how serious is it?"

"Um, actually, do you remember Cory Kingman from high school?" Heidi chewed on the inside of her lip as she watched her mother's reaction. First a scrunch of the brow, then a purse of the lips. Finally, the question.

"Your debate partner?"

"That's the one."

Her mother walked to the fridge and pulled out a head of lettuce and a tomato. "I knew you had a crush on him in school, but I thought he moved away."

"He did, and he joined the Army. Now, he's stationed in Tacoma. Do you want some help with that?" Heidi asked as her mother turned to grab a cutting board and knife. Perhaps sharing her news would be easier if she had something to keep her hands busy.

"No, I've got this," her mother said. "So, you two reconnected?"

Well, that was one way of putting it, Heidi thought. "Yeah, he saw me on the show and when he realized I lived close, he looked me up and showed up at my school."

"Oh, that's nice," her mother said as she began slicing through the head of lettuce. "So, are you two dating now?"

Heidi pursed her lips. Did she tell her mother now? "Is Dad around? I'd rather discuss this with both of you at the same time."

"Of course, he's in the vineyard. Lunch should be ready in a minute anyway. Do you want to go get him and then we can discuss it while we eat?"

Heidi nodded. Sharing her information over lunch

might be better. At least her mother wouldn't be holding a knife then. Not that she thought her mother would get violent, but she didn't want her to injure herself in shock or surprise at the news. Besides, maybe a short stroll in the fresh air would focus her thoughts.

There had never been much of a backyard growing up; the vineyard had taken most of it, but her father had installed a swing set one year when she was younger, and it still sat there rusted and gray now instead of the silver it had once been. The swings swayed slightly in the breeze, emitting a soft creaking that carried on the air like a whisper. Heidi wondered why her father had never removed the set. Had he just never taken the time? Or was this a subtle hint that they still hoped for grandchildren? Would Bella fill that hole for them even though she wasn't blood?

"Dad?" It seemed silly to call out for him. The vineyard was large, and she had no idea where he was or if he would have his phone with him, so she was surprised when his voice carried back to her.

"Over here."

She scanned the area to her left where his voice had come from and saw a flash of movement in between the vines. A few minutes later, she found him, adjusting one of the vines and examining the grapes on it.

He looked up as she approached. "Hey, honey, how are you?"

"I'm good, Dad, how are you?"

"Better than I deserve," he said with a wry smile.

Heidi chuckled softly. That had been her dad's catchphrase for as long as she could remember. He always said it kept him humble, reminded him who was really in charge. "That's good. Mom said lunch is almost ready."

"Good, my stomach was starting to complain a little." He patted the slight swell of his belly. Her father had never been overweight that she could remember, but he had put on a little fluff in the last few years, mainly right about the middle.

"You didn't come all the way out here just for lunch though, did you?" he asked as he took her arm and began walking back toward the house.

"No, though I'm always up for some of Mom's good home cooking. I actually have some news to share."

He narrowed his eyes at her but said nothing more. He knew she would share the information when she was ready. It was one thing she loved about her relationship with her father.

After washing up, they gathered around the table, prayed, and began passing the food in a clockwise direction.

"So, are you going to tell us your news now?" Heidi's mother asked as she passed the bowl of salad.

Heidi took a deep breath, looked from one parent to the other, and said, "I'm getting married." She'd thought about easing into the news, but throwing it out there seemed quicker and easier.

"What?" The word was almost deafening as it exploded from both her mother and father at the same time.

"I'm marrying Cory Kingman in two weeks," Heidi said and dropped her eyes to her plate as she waited for the verbal onslaught that was coming.

"Two weeks?" her mother asked. "I thought you said you just reconnected."

"Wait, who's Cory Kingman?" her father asked.

"Her debate partner from high school," her mother answered. "Why are you rushing into a marriage with him? Are you pregnant?"

Heat seared Heidi's cheeks. "No, I'm not pregnant. It's not like that. Cory is a widower with a young daughter. He just found out he's getting deployed, and he has no one to care for Bella. So, we're getting married."

Her parents stared at her, their shocked faces a blanket of silence that made the room feel unnatural and cold.

"Honey, that's not a reason to marry someone," her father finally said.

"I know, Dad, but I didn't come to this decision lightly."

"How could he even ask that of you?" her mother interrupted, indignation dripping in her voice.

"We made a silly pact in high school," Heidi said,

trying to explain. "When he received his orders, he remembered seeing me on TV and reached out."

"What kind of a pact?" her father asked.

"To marry each other if we weren't married by the age of thirty." It sounded so stupid when it came from her lips, but Heidi still firmly believed she was doing the right thing.

"But he's been married, and you're not thirty yet," her mother said.

"I know, Mom." Heidi tried to keep her exasperation in check. Why did everyone tell her this as if she didn't know? "Look, he asked me, and I told him I would think about it. Then I spent some time with Bella, and she does need someone. Cory is my friend, and I can help him. So I am."

"But helping a friend is not why God created marriage," her father said.

"I know that too, Dad, but I promise I prayed about this for a long time before I made my decision. It may not be the intention, but many marriages in the Bible were arranged or formed out of convenience, and God was still able to bless them and use them. I feel peace about this."

Silence fell on the conversation as her parents exchanged glances. Finally, her father sighed. "You're right," he said, "God does work in mysterious ways. This isn't what I had hoped for you, but if you feel it is the right thing to do, then I support you."

"Thanks, Dad. I appreciate that." Heidi smiled at her father before turning to her mother and lifting an eyebrow in question.

"Oh, all right, I suppose I can support you too. After all, we aren't losing a daughter; we're gaining a son and a granddaughter, right?" Though her mother's smile was small and forced, Heidi knew she was trying to be supportive.

Heidi grinned and sighed as the weight lifted from her shoulders. The future might not always be easy, but if she had her parents on her side, she knew she could do anything.

14

CORY

"Why are we going dress shopping, Daddy?" Bella asked as he helped her put on her shoes.

He sighed and pulled over a chair so he could sit across from her. "Bella, do you know how sometimes your friends' mom or dad has to go away for a few months and do work in another country?"

She nodded, her eyes wide but not quite filled with the understanding he knew would hit her soon.

"Well, unfortunately, the Army decided that it's my turn to do that."

She blinked at him a moment as she processed the information. Then her eyes grew bigger. "But who will take care of me while you're gone?"

Cory picked up her tiny hands and held them in his.

"That is why we're going dress shopping. You know my friend Heidi?"

Bella nodded.

"Well, she has agreed to marry me so that she can take care of you while I'm gone."

Wrinkles erupted across Bella's forehead as her face scrunched in confusion. "So, she's going to be my new mommy?"

"Sort of," Cory said. "She'll take care of you like a mommy, but she'll never replace your first mommy. Mommy will always live here in our hearts." He let go of one of her hands to place his hand across his heart.

"But what happens when you get back? Will she still be my mommy?"

Cory knew couples divorced for less these days, but he didn't want to instill the idea that marriage was disposable in his daughter. "We will still be married when I get back, so yes, she'll still be your mommy."

Bella's lips pursed as her head tilted first one way and then the other. Finally, she shrugged. "Okay, but why do I need a new dress?"

Cory chuckled. If only everyone was as easygoing as his daughter. Of course, there would probably be hard times in the future, but it made him feel better that she seemed to be taking this news in stride. "You need a new dress because Heidi and I are going to have a small wedding and you get to be the flower girl."

Her eyes grew even bigger than before as her mouth fell open. "I get to dress up and drop the petals?"

"You do." Cory shook his head at her excitement. If only a child's sense of wonder could follow them into adulthood. When was the last time he got so excited over something so simple?

"Then what are we waiting for? Let's go." She climbed out of the chair and grabbed his hand to tug him to a standing position as well. "Come on, Daddy."

With a laugh, he let himself be pulled toward the front door.

Half an hour later, they were browsing through dresses in a local shop, and Cory was quickly coming to the realization that he was completely out of his element.

"What about this one, Daddy?" she asked as she held up a purple monstrosity that had more beads and sparkles than he'd ever seen in his life. It reminded him of a costume he might see on a kids' show, gaudy and flashy and definitely not wedding material.

"I think that might be a little over the top. What about this one?" He held up a simple pink dress with a bow in the back.

She wrinkled her nose and shook her head. "That's too plain."

Plain? He wondered when his five-year-old daughter had begun thinking about being plain. "I'll tell you what. Heidi is visiting her parents this weekend, so how about we take pictures of the ones you like and I'll send them to her? She can decide which one fits what she's looking for and then I can come back and get it. Sound good?"

Bella thought for a moment but finally nodded. "Okay, but I'm trying on *all* the ones I like," she said, emphasizing the word all.

Cory bit back his sigh. He had no idea how long that might take, but at least she seemed satisfied by the compromise.

As the sales woman helped Bella take the dresses to a room, Cory found a seat and prepared himself for the fashion show that was about to take place. At least the chair was comfortable. He had no doubt he was in for a good half hour of modeling.

Her first number was the purple monstrosity which looked a little better on but Cory knew Heidi would definitely shake her head at it. He snapped the picture anyway. The second number was a nice blue dress with a shiny top and a sash around the waist, but he was fairly certain Heidi had wanted the girls in pink and the boys in blue. Perhaps he should have discussed colors with her more.

After modeling twenty dresses, Bella finally grew tired of the game and decided she'd had enough. Cory thanked the sales lady, promising to return when he knew which dress to get.

"How about we go get some ice cream?" Cory asked as they exited the dress shop.

Immediately Bella's energy seemed to refill, and she bounced on her toes. "Yes!" She punched her arm up in the air and danced a little jig as they crossed the parking lot. "Can I get chocolate?"

"Of course you can." Cory clicked the button to unlock the car and made a mental note to send Heidi all the pictures he had taken.

15

HEIDI

*T*he next two weeks flew by in a flurry of activity. Not only did school start, which consumed most of her day, but her evenings were spent packing and planning for the wedding. Cory had sent her darling pictures of Bella trying on several dresses, and she had responded with her favorite dress - a cute pink number with a flowy skirt. The few flowers needed had been ordered, and the caterer and bakery had assured her that morning that everything was ready.

The assurances did nothing to calm the butterflies fluttering around in her stomach as she stared at herself in the mirror. She had picked a simple white dress with a lace overlay and a sparkly ornamental decoration under the bodice, but even its beauty was amplified by the soft curls of her auburn hair floating against her bare shoulders.

"You look beautiful," Linley said, appearing in the mirror behind her and slightly adjusting the veil that trailed down Heidi's back.

"I can't believe it's finally happening," Heidi said as she met her friend's eyes in the mirror. The engagement certainly hadn't been a long one, but in a few moments, she would not only have a new name but a new residence and a new stepdaughter. Even though she still believed she was doing the right thing, it was certainly a lot to take in.

"It's not too late to back out if you're having second thoughts," Linley said. Her hands rested on Heidi's shoulders in a gesture of comfort and security.

Heidi shook her head. "No, I still think I'm doing the right thing. It's just a lot of change."

"It is." Linley nodded sagely as she moved her hands to smooth down her pink satin dress, "But, it's nothing you can't handle. You, Heidi Brighton, are a remarkable woman, and you always take things in stride with grace and elegance. I have no doubt you will do the same here."

Heidi blinked and dabbed at the corner of her eyes as moisture filled them. She had promised herself she would not cry today, but how could she not with Linley saying things like that?

"No crying," Linley said, shaking her head. "We spent too much time on your makeup for that. Besides, according to my watch, it's almost time. How about we go find your flower girl and get ready to walk down that aisle?"

Heidi took one last deep breath, grabbed her bouquet, and nodded.

They found Bella in a room down the hall regaling Heidi's mother with her latest tricks and songs she'd been learning in school. Though the two had only met on one other occasion, they had appeared to become fast friends which only amplified Heidi's feelings that this was right and that everything would be okay.

"Is it time?" Bella asked, rushing to Heidi's side and bouncing up and down in her pink satin shoes.

"It is. Are you ready?"

"Yep." She bounded over to a table that held a basket of pink and white flower petals. "I was practicing all yesterday with cut up paper. I'm going to be a pro at this."

Linley, Heidi, and her mother all exchanged amused smiles. "I'm sure you will be," Linley said. "Well, shall we go show everyone how good you are?"

Bella nodded and proudly led the way out of the room. Her little shoulders were pulled back as if on a string and though not haughty, her nose lifted confidently in the air.

At the door to the reception area, Heidi's mother leaned in and hugged her before slipping inside and to her seat. Moments later, the sound of the music started and Linley held the door open for Bella. The two women smiled as they watched the girl take clear deliberate steps down the aisle and carefully drop petals on both sides in an effort to keep them even.

Just before Bella reached the stage, Linley turned to Heidi. "I just wanted to tell you," she said, her eyes soft and serious, "that I think you are doing the right thing too."

"You do?" Heidi wouldn't have changed her mind even if Linley had said the opposite, but hearing confirmation that she was doing the right thing eased the nervous knot in her stomach slightly.

"I do. I think you are brave and selfless, and that little girl is lucky to have you. As is Cory." She looked toward the front of the stage and then back to Heidi. "I just hope he realizes it one day and you two have the marriage you deserve."

Again Heidi felt the water well in her eyes, but she was determined not to smudge her makeup. Instead, she pursed her lips together and pulled her friend in for an impromptu hug before letting her walk down the aisle.

Heidi could see Cory at the front, but she tried to keep her gaze off of him until the music shifted into the traditional wedding march. Though this was not exactly the wedding she'd dreamed of, she could not deny that her heart was racing just as she expected it would. Her feet carried her down the aisle, and though the crowd on either side of her was small, she could feel their eyes on her as she started down the aisle. She could not turn to look at them though. Her eyes seemed locked with Cory's.

He had caught her gaze as she stepped into the small room, and something was in his burning gaze that she had never seen before. Dare she hope that it was feelings? Could he possibly be feeling more than friendship for her the way she was for him? And if he was, was it due only to the wedding or did it run deeper? Could it burrow deep and form a lasting root that would allow them to not only have a comfortable marriage but a happy one?

"You look beautiful," he whispered as he took her hands after she handed her bouquet to Linley.

Warmth flowed up her cheeks and neck, and Heidi knew she probably had a blush to match it. "Thank you. You look dashing yourself."

The preacher began to speak then, but though Heidi heard his voice, she could not concentrate on his words. All she could concentrate on was Cory's skin against hers, how different holding his hand felt this time. And then her mind wandered to what came next.

Of course there would be a small reception, but she was thinking even beyond that. What was it going to be like spending the night in his house tonight? Over the last two weeks, she had been there nearly every evening to drop off boxes, unpack her room, and share dinner with them, but what would it be like to sleep in that room knowing he was just down the hall? Would they stay up late chatting about the wedding? Would he excuse himself and retire early?

"Heidi, please repeat after me."

The sound of the preacher's voice halted her mind's wandering amble, and she forced herself to focus on his words so she could repeat them. She smiled as Cory did the same and wondered if the gleam in his eye told of his struggle to pay attention as well.

"Then by the power vested to me by God and the state of Washington, I now pronounce you husband and wife. You may kiss the bride."

Heidi's eyes widened and her body went still. They hadn't discussed the kiss. How could they have forgotten to discuss the one thing that every wedding had, the thing that people remembered most about a wedding? Were they even going to kiss? What if it was awful? Or perhaps worse, what if it was amazing?

Cory's eyes held a similar deer-in-headlights glaze for a minute. Then, he blinked and the corners of his lips twitched. His shoulder lifted just slightly as if silently saying, "what the heck," and before she could react, his lips were on hers.

Linley had been right when she'd called Heidi a hopeless romantic. Heidi loved to watch romances and bask in the feelings the characters portrayed and imagine what her own heart would feel like when it found that special someone, but as many times as she had imagined the perfect kiss, she had not even come close to what she was feeling now.

Her lips buzzed as if the very touch of his lips had transferred new life to them. A tremor tiptoed down her spine and to her toes sending a conflicting feeling of cold and warmth at the same time through her body. She wanted nothing more than to wrap her arms around his neck and pull him even closer, but the cognizant part of her whispered that now was not the time. However, she could not convince her mouth of that, and when her lips parted, he did not pull back but seemed to pursue even more from her.

Suddenly, as if also realizing reality, he pulled back and Heidi was immediately consumed with how much she missed the sensation. An urge to pull him close to her once again thundered through her, but she squeezed his hands instead. He smiled at her as the congregation around them cheered, but his smile was different. She could almost see the war his mind was engaging in play across his lips. For her, that kiss had solidified her feelings. She could only hope it had done something similar for him.

16

CORY

*C*ory forced his eyes to remain on the aisle as he led Heidi out of the small church. He knew if he looked at her right now, it would be the end of him. Feelings that he'd never experienced for her, never expected with her, surged through him, but surely it was just the moment. He'd seen it before with women who were attracted to men in uniform. They would throw themselves at the men, convince themselves they were in love, but then wake up to the reality of military life and leave. Though he had no intention of leaving Heidi, he had to be feeling something similar, right?

The reception was to take place in the small meeting hall attached to the chapel, and Cory led them that direction. "Well, I guess that's it." He didn't even know what he meant by that, but he seemed unable to stop the words. The need to fill the silence bubbled over.

"What's it?" Heidi asked, confusion coloring her voice and forming tiny lines across her forehead.

"The wedding. It's over. We did it." He wanted to slap his hand over his mouth. He not only sounded like a rambling idiot but like the ceremony they had just gone through had been more of a checklist than a wedding with any real feelings or emotions attached. "I'm sorry. I just mean-" He stopped; he didn't know what he meant. Nor did he know how to convey the confusion that rippled inside him.

"I get it," she said, squeezing his hand. "It feels weird because it's not how we would have done it if we were a real couple."

Yes, it was that, but it wasn't as well. It did feel different because they hadn't planned it as long as most couples did and because they'd entered with different expectations. At least he had. But it also felt very much the same as his marriage to Desiree had. The same sense of excitement flooded his veins, the same nervousness over what happened next pounded in his chest. But with that was another new feeling. Something he couldn't explain. Something that had sprouted when he kissed Heidi.

They'd forgotten to discuss the kiss. Perhaps it would have been different if they'd practiced beforehand. Perhaps he would have been able to remove the feelings if they hadn't kissed for the first time in the church, with people watching, with her looking like an angel. Or perhaps it wouldn't have been different at all. Perhaps, he'd been fooling himself trying to deny that he had no feelings for her other than friendship.

The last two weeks with her coming over in the evenings had been the happiest weeks he'd had in a long time. Some of that came from watching Bella respond to her. Seeing his daughter laughing and smiling more often sent his heart soaring, but some of it had nothing to do with Bella. And that was the part he was wrestling with now. He loved Heidi, but he wasn't in love with her. Was he? Was he really ready to open his heart again?

"We could take a walk around the chapel to give everyone time to get to the reception if you'd like," he offered. In truth, he hoped the fresh air might clear his head and give him a new perspective, so he was delighted when she agreed.

He kept a hold of her hand as he opened the door. They'd held hands before, but this time felt different. However, it also felt natural and right, and he needed something that felt right to hold onto - to ground himself.

"The fall is always so pretty in Washington," Heidi said as they walked across burnt red and orange leaves that crinkled softly under their steps. Tiny pink petals - cherry blossoms - floated in the air as they fell from the tree in a lazy pattern.

"Yes, it is." He couldn't remember the last time he'd paid attention to the fall - to the colors or the breeze.

"Do you miss it when you leave?"

He never had before. He'd missed his wife and his daughter, his car, and the ability to do the activities he was used to doing, but he'd never missed the fall before. Somehow, he thought that this time, he might.

"I'm not sure I ever thought about it before, but it certainly won't be this pretty where I go." He thought back to the last deployment. To the oppressive heat and the never-ending sea of colorless sand. To the constant fear of bombs that created sleepless nights and exhausted days.

"I can't imagine how hard it will be," Heidi said, stopping to turn and grab his other hand as well. "Whatever I can do to make it more bearable, I will. Just tell me."

A burst of warmth erupted in his chest. He had missed this kind of connection, especially since Desiree had gotten sick. Cory knew his daughter loved him and would do anything for him, but she was five. There was something different about another adult having his back, promising to support him in any way possible. But even that, he could get from his brothers-in-arms. What he couldn't get from them, what he hadn't realized he missed until this very moment was that connection from a woman, the look that blazoned in Heidi's eyes, the feel of her soft hands in his.

"I will," he said, clearing his throat to suppress the emotions he was battling. He would have to process all of these feelings later, but now was not the time. In fact, it was probably time for them to head back into the building and attend their reception. "We can talk about that later though. We should probably head back inside."

Heidi hesitated a moment as though she wanted to protest, but then she nodded. "You're probably right, and we have a few more days to figure it out, right?"

"Right." A few more days. That was all they had, and while leaving was never easy, Cory felt this time would be even harder than normal. Determined not to focus on the dreaded day ahead, Cory pulled back his shoulders, squeezed her hand, and led them back to the building where the reception would be held.

"You ready?" he asked as they reached the main door.

"I'm starving," Heidi said with a chuckle, "does that count?"

"I am too," Cory said with a grin as he pulled open the door.

"And here they are, Sergeant and Mrs. Cory Kingman." The voice of the DJ - one of Cory's men who had worked at a radio station in college and knew how to work a sound system - blared out over the speakers as they entered the room. It was nothing lavish, but Cory appreciated what had been done. Circular tables draped in white tablecloths and topped with a display of flowers surrounded the small dance floor. The catered food sat along two long tables near the far wall, and servers dressed in black and white stood behind the tables, ready to serve. White Christmas lights twined with ribbons and streamers hung from the ceiling in lazy loops casting a soft romantic glow about the small room.

"It's beautiful," Heidi whispered beside him.

He wanted to tell her that it was not nearly as beautiful as she was - he was still floored by how pretty she looked today - but before he could say anything, Bella came running up to them.

"Daddy, did you see me toss the petals? I was so good, wasn't I?"

Cory laughed as he leaned down to scoop up Bella. "You were indeed, bug. Guess that practice paid off, huh?"

She nodded. "And I kept my dress clean. I really like my dress, but it's not nearly as pretty as yours Ms. Heidi. Someday I hope I can wear a dress like that."

Cory knew it was harmless little girl talk, but the idea of his daughter being old enough to marry was not one he wanted to think about. Nor was the idea that she would get married without her mother there. At least she would have Heidi. It wouldn't be the same, but he knew Heidi would love Bella as if she were her own, and she would help the girl with whatever issues arose in the future.

"I think your dress is prettier than mine," Heidi said with a wink, "but I'll tell you what, if you really like my dress, I'll have it preserved for you so maybe you can wear it one day."

Bella's eyes grew large. "Really? That would be awesome! Now can we eat, Daddy? I'm starving."

Cory shook his head at Bella's rapid shift in attention and topic but nodded as he set her down. "I think that's a great idea. Heidi said she was hungry too, so how about we get this party started?"

"Yes." Bella inserted herself between Heidi and Cory, grabbing each of their hands with her own as she led the way to the back tables.

Cory filled his plate and helped Bella with hers as they made their way down the line. After they reached the end, the three returned to the head table where Linley and Tanner sat talking with each other. As they sat down, the flow of congratulations began, and Cory found it hard to find the time to eat his food as he offered smiles and thanks to those who approached. Finally, the buzz around their table quieted, and Cory and Heidi were able to enjoy the food.

She had done an amazing job with the caterer as well. Though the fare was simple, it was delicious and homey. He sneaked a glance at her out of the corner of his eye. Her auburn hair lay in soft spirals against her bare shoulders, and he smiled as he realized he would get to see her like this every day from now on. Well, at least until he had to leave.

"What?" she asked, catching him staring at her. "Do I have something on my face?" Her fingers wiped at her lips and then her chin.

"No," he said with a laugh. "I was just admiring how beautiful you are and what an amazing job you did with all of this, especially on such short notice."

Her cheeks flushed a soft pink color. "Oh, well, thank you." She looked away to scan the room. "It did turn out pretty nice."

"Yes, it did." Cory turned his attention back to his food, but he could not keep his eyes from darting over to Heidi now and then.

When most of the room had finished eating and plates were pushed to the side, the DJ announced the first dance. Cory's heart pounded in his chest as he took Heidi's hand and led her to the dance floor, but he wasn't exactly sure why. Was he worried that people watching might realize they weren't "in love?" That seemed unlikely as most of them understood the need for the rushed marriage. Or was he worried that they might see he was feeling something? He wasn't sure it was love, but he'd never been so affected by Heidi's presence as he was when he pulled her close and wrapped an arm around her lower back.

Her auburn hair smelled of strawberries and vanilla, and it lay on her bare shoulders like rose gold glistening in the sun. A heartbeat pulsed between them, but he wasn't sure if it was hers or his.

"I can't believe we pulled this off," she said as she looked up at him. One of her hands was encased firmly in his, but her other lay on his shoulder. Though her touch was soft, he was keenly aware of her hand's presence, and he wondered what her hands would feel like on his face? In his hair?

"Yeah, you did a wonderful job," he said, trying to bring his focus back to the moment at hand. It was not easy as his mind kept straying to what was to come. He'd always enjoyed being around Heidi, but now he was having a hard time focusing on anything other than kissing her again. Plus, what would it be like with Heidi staying in his house tonight? They had seemed to integrate well so far, but that had only been for short spans of time - a few hours. Now, she would be there every day. Would they still mesh as well?

"Thank you, but I didn't do it alone. I do want to thank you for this though. For having the wedding. I know it was a lot to get done especially with everything else on your mind, but it means a lot to me."

You mean a lot to me. The words exploded in his mind, begging to be said aloud, but when he opened his mouth, they did not come out. Instead, he said, "You're welcome." You're welcome? What was wrong with him?

As he watched her smile falter slightly, he wanted to

explain, to try again, but he couldn't. Fear paralyzed him. Fear that what he was feeling wasn't real. Fear that she wouldn't feel the same way. But most of all, fear that she would and then this would all come crashing down around him, and he wouldn't be able to survive a second broken heart.

17

HEIDI

*T*he mood was different as Heidi, Cory, and Bella returned home that evening after the ceremony. Not bad necessarily but definitely different. Heidi had been sure that Cory felt something during the wedding, something more than friendship. It had certainly felt like that during the kiss and the walk outside after. Even when he'd taken her in his arms for the first dance, she'd been sure that there was something, but then suddenly he'd shut down. Instead of telling her he cared, he just said "you're welcome" and then it was like a wall had shot up between them.

Thankfully, Bella had been too tired to notice. After wearing herself out dancing at the reception and stuffing her face full of rich food, she had passed out in the car on the drive home, and now slumbered in Cory's arms as Heidi pushed the door open.

"I'm going to put her in bed," Cory said.

"Sure, do you want any help?" Heidi asked. It felt weird now - this conversation, being in his house knowing that she would be sleeping here tonight, not knowing what was going on in his head, all of it.

"No, I'm good, but if you want, we can watch a movie or something when I'm done?" Cory stumbled over the words as if he too was unsure of where they stood now. Heidi wondered if this was their new normal. Had they lost their comfortable repertoire now? And if so, would they ever be able to overcome it?

"Sure, sounds good. I'll make some popcorn." She wasn't really hungry after the food they'd had a few hours earlier, but she needed something to do, something to keep her hands busy and her mind off how nervous she suddenly felt.

Cory nodded and disappeared down the hallway. Heidi made her way to the kitchen. After eating here nearly every night with them for the past few weeks, she knew where all the food was. She opened the cupboard and took out a bag of popcorn, placed it in the microwave, and hit the button for three minutes. But now what?

Her insides churned like a ship adrift in the ocean. With one bob, there would be excitement about this new journey, but then she would come off that wave and wonder if they could really make this work.

The sound of Cory's approaching footsteps reached her just before the microwave beeped.

"That smells good," he said as he entered the kitchen.

"Yeah, it does," Heidi said as she opened the microwave and retrieved the bag. She'd always loved the smell of popcorn - the comfort and homey feeling it created - but tonight her nerves were stronger than the smell.

"So, today went well, I think," Cory said as Heidi retrieved a bowl and poured the popcorn in.

"It was beautiful," Heidi said. "Thank you again."

"Of course. I'm glad we did it, and I know Bella really enjoyed it." He led the way to the living room as if nothing was wrong, but Heidi had heard the forced brightness in his voice. "What do you feel like watching?"

"Um, anything but a horror movie," Heidi said as she claimed one corner of the couch. Normally her love of romances ran deep, but suddenly it felt odd asking for one. Would he think she was trying to make a move? That she was asking for more romance? In a way, he wouldn't be wrong. That kiss had rocked her world, and she still felt heat grace her cheeks every time she thought about it. But... she didn't know what he thought. There'd been almost no touch since the dance. She could just ask him, but though they'd once been close friends, posing that question suddenly felt awkward. She bit the inside of her lip as he pulled up a movie app on the TV. Would it always be this way?

"How about a comedy?" Cory asked. "I think there's a pretty good one that just came out."

"Sure."

He started the movie and then sat down on the other end of the couch. Stifling a sigh, she placed the popcorn in between them. It wasn't a large distance, but with the state of her nerves, it felt like an ocean separated them.

Heidi tried to pay attention to the movie, but her brain wouldn't focus. Instead, it replayed the wedding in her mind, searching for any clue, any detail that might tell her what Cory was feeling. But there was nothing concrete. There was the kiss, but it would have been odd if they hadn't kissed at the wedding. There was the walk around the building afterwards, and there was the first dance. The dance where at first she'd thought he was going to tell her that he felt something more than friendship as well, but he hadn't. And now they were here. Confused and silent and ignoring the giant elephant in the room.

"Well," he said when the movie finished, "that was good, huh?"

"Yeah." Heidi wasn't sure what else to say. The silence between them hung like an uncomfortable, invisible curtain. "Well, I guess I'll get ready for bed."

"Yeah." Cory turned off the TV, stood, and shoved his hands in his pockets. "I guess it is getting late."

"It is." Heidi grabbed the bowl as she stood, preparing to take it back to the kitchen, but as she moved, so did Cory. Then they both paused.

"You go first," he said, motioning with his hand, looking as nervous and unsure as Heidi felt.

"Thanks." She led the way to the kitchen, surprised when he followed her. She'd been sure he would have just gone to bed. Turning on the water, she rinsed the bowl and left it in the sink to wash in the morning.

"I can wash that later," Cory said, stepping close behind her.

"Thanks, but I can wash it in the morning too." Heidi turned to grab a paper towel from the counter, but instead, she turned right into Cory's chest. His arms reached up to steady her, but all they succeeded in doing was sending tingles shooting down to her toes again. She looked up at him, unsure of what to do, to say.

For a moment they simply stared at each other, electricity crackling in the air between them. Heidi's lips parted - she wanted to kiss him again, to wrap her arms around his neck and pull him closer, but she couldn't. Not until she knew he felt the same. Because right now, they at least still had friendship - an awkward and stilted friendship at the moment - but if she made a move and Cory didn't reciprocate, even that friendship might fade away. Then they would be two strangers just existing, and she didn't want that.

Cory dropped his hands and stepped back. "How about whoever gets up first gets it?"

"Sure." A feeling of defeat surged through Heidi as she nodded. "Guess I'll get to bed then."

He returned her nod and took another step back, allowing her access to the hallway. Swallowing the lump growing in her throat, Heidi pulled her shoulders back and held her head high as she walked to her room.

When the door closed behind her, she let the emotions overwhelm her. Even though she'd known the marriage was fake and had thought she'd prepared herself for that outcome, actually living through it was another matter and much harder than she'd thought it would be. It had to get easier right?

As she changed into pajamas and climbed into bed, the thought that perhaps it would always be like this pounded in her head. Closing her eyes, she did the only thing she could do. She gave it over to God.

18

CORY

*C*ory sighed as he walked to his bedroom. He knew Heidi was confused. It was written all over her face, and he wanted to say something to her, something to make it better, but he was confused too. And he had no idea how to make it better.

He flicked on his light and stared at his bed. After his marriage to Desiree, she'd shared his bed. At first, it had been hard getting used to someone else in the bed with him. There was the loss of space, the accidental colliding of limbs, and of course the sound of another person breathing and sometimes snoring in the night. But he'd gotten used to it. Then she'd gotten sick and he'd taken to sleeping in the nearby chair so as not to disturb her. Only when she'd passed had he returned to the bed, and then it had been weird to have it all to himself.

Now he was married again, but Heidi wasn't sharing his bed. She was down the hall in another bed, in another room which also felt strange.

He ran a hand across his forehead. This was definitely more awkward than he had expected it would be, but surely it would get better. If not in the few days before he left then after he returned. By then, Heidi would be established in the house and he would be the one feeling more like a guest.

After brushing his teeth and changing into sleepwear, he climbed into his bed, but his mind refused to settle. He flicked on the television, hoping something would grab his attention and distract him from the thoughts careening around in his head. Unfortunately, it was late and there was not much on. He flipped past an old rerun, past the news, past a sporting event being aired for the second time and somehow, he landed on a religious channel.

The man, dressed smartly in a tie and a suit coat, did not stand at a large pulpit as most of the televangelists Cory had seen before did. Instead, he sat at a table and spoke directly to the camera as if he was speaking to the viewers at home.

"These are troubling times we are in," he said in a soft sincere voice, "but there is hope. Jesus said that He is our hope and that He will take care of our troubles if we cast them onto Him. We all know that, but for some reason, we like to think that our problems are too small for Him to care. We think that we can handle the little things and we'll let God handle the big things. However, nothing is too small for God, and if we let Him handle the little things, we'll have fewer of the big things."

The man continued to speak, but Cory no longer heard the words. Was that what he should do with these feelings for Heidi? Give them to God? He'd stopped talking to God when Desiree died, believing that God had abandoned him, but maybe he'd simply been looking at it in the wrong way.

Flicking off the television, he stared up at the ceiling. A part of him wanted to call out to God, to ask Him to help with Heidi, but the stubborn part of him insisted there was no God or if there was that He didn't care. After all, He'd let Desiree die. He'd taken her from him and left Bella without a mother. Except...had He? Heidi wasn't Desiree, but Cory knew she would be an amazing mother to Bella.

He shook his head and closed his eyes. It was too much to think about tonight. He'd do it tomorrow. Tomorrow when the sun was up, things would be clearer. They'd have to be.

BELLA AND HEIDI were already dressed and eating breakfast in the kitchen when Cory joined them the next morning.

"Hi, Daddy, are you going to go to church with us today?" Bella asked, looking up from her cereal.

"Uh…" Cory had forgotten it was Sunday.

"I'm sure your daddy has a lot to do to get ready for his deployment," Heidi said, jumping to his rescue.

Bella's lips pushed out in a small pout. "But this is the last Sunday you'll be here, right? You should come with us at least once. Besides, I want to spend all the time with you that I can, and I have to go to school tomorrow."

"How about we all stay home then?" Heidi suggested. "You and I can have a little Bible study while Daddy packs and then you can hang out with him afterwards."

"No, it's fine," Cory said. "When would we have to leave?"

"Half an hour."

"Okay, let me get some coffee and breakfast. Then I'll grab a quick shower and be good to go."

"Are you sure?" Heidi asked. "I don't want to mess with your time."

"I want to go," he said. He must have been convincing this time because she merely nodded and returned to drinking her own coffee.

"Yay, I'm so glad, Daddy. I can show you my

classroom and you can meet my teacher. She's not as nice as Ms. Fields, but she's still nice."

Cory nodded as he poured his cup. He couldn't believe he had just agreed to go to church, but maybe it wouldn't be so bad.

19

HEIDI

*H*eidi stared at the ID card that now gave her access to come and go freely on the base. It looked like the temporary paper one she'd been given except that this one was hard like a driver's license or a credit card and had her new last name on it. Heidi Kingman. It still felt a little surreal seeing that name in print. She hadn't even changed it at school yet. Though she'd considered it, she had decided to wait until the next school year to officially go by Mrs. Kingman. Learning her name once was hard enough for four- and five-year olds; she didn't want to make them learn a different one just weeks into the school year.

"You ready?" Cory asked.

"Um, yeah." Heidi tucked the card in her wallet and stood. Linley had offered to watch Bella for a few hours for them after school so that she and Cory could hammer out the last of the details needed before his deployment. They'd already taken care of the will and the power of attorney. The ID card had been the last stop.

"I can't believe I have to leave tomorrow," Cory said as they exited the office building and descended the concrete steps.

"Me either. These last few days have felt like a whirlwind and they've been hard enough with you here. I have to admit that I'm a little scared how much harder it will be when you're gone."

Cory grabbed her hand and turned her to him. She looked down at their hands. It was the first time they'd really touched since the wedding. They'd been tiptoeing around each other for the last few days, and even at church the previous Sunday, he'd sat rigidly with his hands firmly in his lap.

"You are a strong and independent woman," he said. "The next few months will be hard, but you will do great."

She lifted her eyes to find Cory staring intently at her. "Thank you. Knowing that you have faith in me helps me have faith too."

"I've always had faith in you."

Heidi felt the electricity crackle in the air between them, and her lips parted. His eyes dropped to her lips and then back up to her eyes, and she took a step closer to him.

"Cory," she began, but before she could continue, his phone went off.

"Sorry, hang on." As he let go of her hand to answer his phone, she knew the moment was gone. Whatever had been about to happen between them would be gone when his call ended. Just like all the moments before them.

"Yes, sir. Okay, sir. Thank you."

"Everything okay?" she asked when he ended the call.

"Yeah, I guess there's just something I forgot to pick up. Can we stop by work really quick before we go get Bella?"

"Of course." Heidi waited for him to grab her hand again, but just as she'd suspected, the moment was gone. She swallowed her sigh, but she wondered if they would ever have another moment again.

20

CORY

*C*ory could not believe the day of his departure was already here. It had been an interesting few days from the high of the wedding to the lows of getting used to having Heidi in his house. It wasn't that he minded her presence, but it felt strange now. As if they were walking on eggshells around each other. As if they were more than friends but not really lovers. He thought from time to time that she felt the same. Her eyes would linger on his or focus on his lips. Accidental touches would slow down time, but neither of them would utter the first word - the word that would start everything in motion or destroy what they had.

He wanted to do it. Especially today. But what was the point? In two hours, he would be boarding a plane and flying across the world for six months. No, it would be better to wait. She and Bella could bond and then he could see how his own heart really felt when he got back. Yes, that was the best idea.

Zipping up his bag, he hoisted it over his shoulder and left the bedroom. Bella stood in the hallway, her face stoic and sad.

"Do you have to go, Daddy?"

He set down the bag to pick her up, relishing the feeling of her in his arms. It was a memory he would have to sear into his mind, so that he could retrieve it and replay it on the lonely days and nights he knew would be ahead. "You know I do, bug, but Heidi will take care of you, and I'll call when I can. It's going to feel long, but I promise, I'll be back before you know it."

She sniffed and nodded, but he could tell she did not believe him. That was okay. He didn't believe himself. He squeezed her tightly and blinked to keep the tears at bay before setting her back down.

"You're going to be brave and help Heidi out, right?" he asked, lifting his bag again and taking her hand in his. So small. He loved serving his country, but this was the part he hated the most. How could he leave someone so small, someone who needed him?

"I'll do my best," she said in a quiet voice.

"You'll do great."

Heidi stood in the kitchen when they entered. Her hands tapped softly against the side of her leg as if she wasn't sure what to do with them, but she jumped to attention when she spotted them. "Ready?" she asked.

Could he ever really be ready? "As I can be," he said with a soft sigh. Their eyes caught and held for a moment. In them, he could see her hesitation and fear. He wished he could tell her that everything was going to be all right, but he knew the next few months would be hard on her. However, he would work hard on being there for her as much as he could.

Breaking their eye contact, Heidi grabbed the keys from the counter and led the way to the front door. Bella clung to his hand as if it were a lifeboat in a troubled sea, but Cory didn't mind. He would miss getting to hold her hand.

When they reached the car, he helped Bella into her seat, but she whimpered when he tried to let go of her. "Sit with me, Daddy," she said with big doe eyes that looked as if they might spout a river of tears any moment.

Cory glanced to Heidi, wanting desperately to spend the time he could with his daughter but not wanting Heidi to feel like a chauffeur. Thankfully, she didn't seem to take it as a slight. Instead, she offered a tight smile and a small nod to let him know she understood.

"Okay, baby, I'm going to sit with you, but you do have to let go of me first."

She pressed her lips together and shook her head.

"Bella, I promise. I'll sit right there." Cory pointed at

the empty seat next to her. Finally, he felt her grip lessen on his hand. It didn't, however, lessen the grip on his heart. Stepping back, he shut her door before reaching up to wipe away the tear trickling out of the corner of his eye. He couldn't let her see him cry. He needed to be strong. For her, for Heidi, for himself.

He pulled back his shoulders, loaded his bag, and then climbed back in beside Bella. When he was buckled in, Heidi started the car and headed toward the hangar he would be departing from.

Silence filled the car as they drove, but it was not the comfortable silence that he normally felt with Bella or even Heidi. Things had been more strained between them the last few days, but it had never felt like this. This silence was suffocating, like a thick fog that invaded your throat and squeezed your lungs, making it painful to draw a breath.

When Heidi parked the car and the engine stilled, Cory knew the time to say goodbye had come. He knew they had to walk into the hangar, hug, and try to cram the next six months into a few minutes. He knew it had to happen, but every bone in his body screamed that he should stay, that there had to be another way, that he couldn't leave Bella alone for that long. She couldn't lose both parents.

Cory took a deep breath to try and slow the pounding

of his heart. This was his job, and he had to do it. No matter how hard it was. "Okay, time to go."

Bella pursed her lips and shook her head, squeezing Cory's hand even tighter. Though he kept his face stoic, inside his heart broke into a million tiny pieces. He hated that he was causing his daughter so much pain.

Suddenly, the door behind Bella opened, and Heidi's face appeared. "Come on, Bella, we can be strong girls for Daddy, right?"

Bella looked up at Heidi and then back at Cory before nodding. "Okay."

As Heidi began to unbuckle Bella to remove her from the seat, Cory exited from the other side and grabbed his bag from the back. He slung it over his shoulder, and by the time he made it around the side, Bella was out and firmly gripping Heidi's hand. She grabbed his hand as well when he reached her, and the three began the slow walk into the hangar.

Their footsteps echoed off the concrete floor of the large hangar as they entered. A few other families were scattered around, all huddled together as Cory knew they would be shortly, and a somber feeling floated in the air.

Cory led the way to a few open chairs and dropped his bag before squatting down to be eye-to-eye with Bella. "I know you're sad and probably afraid, baby, but I promise Heidi will take good care of you."

"I know, Daddy, but I still don't want you to go."

Cory pulled Bella to his chest and wrapped his arms around her. "I know, bug, and I don't want to go either, but I have to. I promise I'll call when I can." On previous deployments, Cory had been allowed one phone call a week, so he figured he would at least have that.

Overhead, a loudspeaker sounded, announcing the soldiers needed to move. Cory gave Bella one more squeeze before standing and stepping toward Heidi. Every part of him wanted to kiss her, to tell her how much he would miss her, but he couldn't do it. Something held him back.

He placed a hand on her arm, "Heidi, I..."

"I know," she said with a nod. "You don't have to say it."

Nodding, he pulled her to him and gave her a hug as well. "I promise I'll keep in touch."

The speaker sounded again, and Cory, after squeezing Bella once more, shouldered his bag, flashed a final wave, and followed his fellow soldiers into the loading area. Just before he turned the corner, he glanced behind him to see Heidi's hands on Bella's shoulders. They waved, but the sadness shone from their faces like a flashlight piercing the darkness. Attempting a smile, he returned the wave and then turned the corner.

21

HEIDI

"How about we go for some ice cream?" Heidi asked as she loaded Bella back up in the car. Tears streamed down the girl's face, and she had long since stopped trying to control her hitching sobs.

"I just... want my... Daddy," she said in a hitching manner.

A feeling of complete helplessness settled on Heidi's shoulders as she hugged the small girl. "I know you do, Bella. I miss him too, but we have to be strong, remember?"

She shook her head and folded her arms across her chest. "I don't want... to be strong...I want my Daddy."

Clearly, this was bigger than ice cream could fix. The only problem was Heidi couldn't fix this issue, and for about the thousandth time, she wondered if she had taken on more than she could handle.

After securing Bella, she climbed into the driver's seat and pointed the car back to the house. Though she lived there now, it wasn't quite home to her yet. The house still felt like someone else lived there. Desiree's touch still lingered in the air, on the furniture, in the decor, but Heidi didn't want to change things too drastically either. There had already been too much change in Bella's life.

Cory's car sat in the driveway when she pulled in, a painful reminder that, even though he was gone, pieces of him would remain all around them as daily reminders. With a sigh, Heidi turned off the car, rescued the still teary-eyed Bella from the backseat, and unlocked the front door. Before she even had the door all the way open, Bella darted inside, running straight to her room and slamming the door behind her. The noise hit Heidi like a slap, and a part of her wanted to remind Bella they didn't slam doors, but the other part of her understood the girl's frustration.

"Don't worry, it will get easier."

Heidi turned at the unfamiliar voice to see a thin woman in a pair of jeans and a bright t-shirt crossing the yard towards her.

"Sorry, I haven't been over sooner, but I've been preparing for this deployment just like you have. I'm Kaci." She stuck out her slender hand and the colorful bangles on her wrist clinked together.

Heidi took the woman's hand, surprised when her grip was firm and strong. "I'm Heidi. Nice to meet you. So, you've been through this before?"

"Oh yeah." Kaci nodded, sending her brown ponytail bobbing behind her. "This is my fourth one. I'd like to tell you they get easier, but..." she shrugged, "they really don't."

If Kaci was trying to reassure her, she was failing miserably. "Oh, that's unfortunate," Heidi said.

"Don't get me wrong," Kaci said with a laugh and a small smile. "You get used to them - the packing, the being a single parent, juggling the kids' activities by yourself, but it never really gets easier."

Heidi sighed. "I'm having a hard enough time just being a parent. Cory and I just recently married, so I haven't even been Bella's stepmother very long. I have to admit it feels a little overwhelming to do it alone now."

"That can be hard, but you aren't alone here. Military bases are like family, and we take care of each other. I'm right next door to you and across the street is Rachelle O'Rear. She's the oldest in our small group. This is her tenth deployment, so she has a lot of knowledge. On the other side of you," she swung her hand in that direction, "is Darby McGill. She's another newlywed like yourself. Just moved in about a year ago, but this is also her first deployment. Anyway, we get together once a week to decompress. Rachelle's daughter watches all the kids upstairs in their game room, and we bring wine. We'd love for you to join us. Monday night at five."

Heidi blinked at the woman who had just unloaded a ton of information in a very short amount of time. "Sure, we'd love to come. I'm sure I'll be ready for some wine by then."

"Girl, we all will. I'll let you get back to what you were doing, but remember, I'm just next door if you need anything."

"Thank you, I appreciate it." Heidi waved goodbye to the woman and entered the house, feeling a sense of hope and relief for the first time all morning. This wouldn't be easy, but now that she knew she had new friends around, it seemed doable.

The house was still quiet as she entered. After locking the door behind her, Heidi moved quietly towards Bella's room. No sound came from within. Heidi knocked softly and when she received no answer, she pushed the door open. Bella lay curled in bed, her stuffed lamb tucked securely under her chin, and her long lashes a contrast to her delicate cheeks.

Heidi supposed she shouldn't be surprised. They'd had to wake up early to get Cory dropped off on time, and Bella, if she was anything like Heidi, probably hadn't slept well the night before either. A yawn escaped Heidi's mouth. She should grab a short nap while she could as well. Who knew what kind of mood Bella would be in when she woke up?

Afraid Bella might think she'd left if she napped in her room, Heidi grabbed her pillow and a blanket before returning to the living room and curling up on the couch. She turned and adjusted and re-adjusted her pillow before finally finding a comfortable spot. "Lord," she whispered, "please give me the strength to do this. Help me to know what Bella needs and to be able to provide it." There was more she needed to say, to ask for, but the words slipped away as her eyes grew heavy and closed.

22

CORY

Cory pulled out the photo he had taken of Bella and Heidi and placed it on the small table beside his cot, now his makeshift bed for the next six months.

"That your family?"

He looked up to see his fellow soldier Ronnie Gunderson leaning down over the side of the top bunk and pointing at the picture. Ronnie had bright red hair that reminded Cory a little of Archie, the comic book character, and a little of Heidi.

"Yeah. That's my daughter Bella, and my..." Cory paused. He had been about to say friend, but he supposed Heidi was more than that now. "My wife." Why did the word still seem so foreign on his tongue?

"They're both beautiful," Ronnie said. He disappeared for a moment and then returned with a picture of his own.

"I got a girl too. Not married yet though. We were hoping to do it before the first deployment, but she didn't want to rush it."

"I can understand that," Cory said. He thought about telling Ronnie his story with Heidi, but he couldn't find the words to make it sound rational. Besides, he didn't know Ronnie well, and it really wasn't any of his business.

"So, is this your first deployment?" Ronnie asked, continuing the conversation.

"No, it's my fourth." It would have actually been his fifth, but the Army had given him a reprieve from the last one as the orders had come down just after Desiree died.

Ronnie let out a low whistle. "Fourth. Wow. So, like, what do we do? Because I have to tell you, I'm already bored."

Cory chuckled as he thought back to his first deployment. He had certainly felt the same way. "Well, every deployment is different," he said, opening the drawer of the table and placing his shirts inside, "but generally, we play cards or watch movies when shift is over. Some places have alcohol tents, but I don't think this one does. Once or twice a week, we're allowed to use the phones to call home, so we try to set up a rotation. That way it's easier for the family back home and no one misses their spot here. Seeing as this area we're in is relatively safe, there will probably be a few excursions into town where you can take pictures and buy souvenirs, but that's about it. Hopefully, you brought some books to read or a device that can play movies or something."

Ronnie's eyes, which had lost their shine during Cory's speech, appeared to light up at the last statement. "Does that mean we have streaming services here, like YouTube?"

"Uh, no." Cory shook his head. He had probably been just like Ronnie a decade ago, but now he wondered how these new soldiers survived. They seemed incapable of reading a book, only able to focus on junk that was fed directly to them through silly gamers and videos.

Ronnie's face fell. "Oh, so you must have meant like DVDs or something."

"Yeah. There's occasionally a library where you can rent some - nothing good, mind you, but better than nothing, but otherwise, it's whatever you brought from home." Cory looked down at his laptop, resting snuggly in his bag with a few boxed sets of TV shows he enjoyed and hadn't had time to catch up on. He supposed that was the one good part of deployments. He certainly had a lot of time. Time to read, time to watch episodes, time to think about how much he missed Bella. And Heidi. Perhaps excess time wasn't so great after all.

"How come no one tells you this stuff at the briefings before deployments?" Ronnie's voice had taken on a glum tone, and his shoulders drooped in defeat.

"I guess because they're more focused on telling you

the things that will save your life rather than relieve your boredom." Cory didn't mean to sound snappish, but the man's attitude bothered him. No one enjoyed deployments, at least no one he knew, but they were a necessary evil. The government paid them extra for the sacrifice. Not that the money mattered, but it was at least a token showing they understood the sacrifice. Yet many of the younger soldiers were just like Ronnie. They didn't understand the sacrifice. They had probably joined for the free college or been persuaded by a buddy who either had a cushy job or regretted his choice and wanted someone else to be miserable with. There were even a few Cory had met who joined simply for the women who seemed to have a thing for men in uniform.

Ronnie said nothing else, but his head disappeared from Cory's view. They would make up in a few days. It was always like that. Tempers flared hot on deployments but they burned brightly and then extinguished. Petty disagreements lost their weight when you realized the men around you might be the only thing keeping you safe.

Cory pulled out his laptop, determined to type up a letter to Heidi and Bella, even if he couldn't send it until he was able to make it to the hall where the internet was available, but as he lifted his laptop, he spied a black book underneath. He didn't remember packing any books - he wasn't much of a reader and when he was, he read them on his phone. Setting the laptop on the bed, he pulled the book out. The Holy Bible. It was his, but he hadn't used it in ages. Not since Desiree's death. Heidi must have snuck it into his bag, but he wasn't angry. Somehow, with the heavy book in his hands, he felt relief. Maybe it was time to give God another chance.

After adjusting his pillow against the wall, Cory leaned back and opened the book. He didn't even know where to begin reading, so he let the book fall open and then scanned the pages.

"But blessed is the one who trusts in the Lord, whose confidence is in him. They will be like a tree planted by the water that sends out its roots by the stream. It does not fear when heat comes; its leaves are always green. It has no worries in a year of drought and never fails to bear fruit." - Jeremiah 17: 7-8

The words resonated in his heart. They pinged and bounced like a pinball in a machine. Could he do that? Could he step back and let God be in control again? He thought back over the last year. It certainly hadn't been much better trying to do it on his own, and honestly, except for Desiree's death, it had been better when he'd been letting God steer the wheel. He wasn't sure he was ready to give up full control, but he felt his grip lessen. God had obviously sent Heidi, and if He'd done that, perhaps He did have a plan.

Cory closed the book. He would think on that, but it was the first day - he was tired and sore and he missed his daughter. Setting the Bible beside him, he opened his laptop and pulled up an email draft. His fingers tapped lightly against the keys as he thought about what to say. He wanted to tell them about his trip, but it was important he keep it light.

Dear Heidi and Bella,

I hope you both are having fun, but not too much without me. I've arrived in the desert. It's definitely not home, but I have set a picture of you on the nightstand next to my bed so I can see you every morning and every evening.

My trip was rather uneventful. I rode on a giant airplane for a long time. Unfortunately, military planes aren't as comfortable as civilian planes, so I didn't get much sleep. I'll definitely sleep well tonight even though this bed is as hard as rock.

I hope the rest of your weekend went well. I'd love to hear about church and school. I know I can't be there every day, but I hope you'll tell me each night how you're doing. I'll try to get internet as much as possible so that I can write back to you each day, and as soon as I get a postal address, I'll send that along too. I miss you both and can't wait till I can give you a big hug again. Guess that's all for now. My lids are growing heavy which means I should probably call it a night before I pass out on my keyboard. I'll write again soon.

Love, Cory

He wondered if he should reword the ending. Would Heidi get the wrong idea if he signed it love? Perhaps he should send an email just for Bella and then another one for Heidi. That seemed silly and unnecessary though. Even though things were still new and different for them, she was his wife now. At least that was something he could hash out while he was here. Before he returned, he needed to figure out not only what Heidi was to him but how they moved forward from here. Again though, a thought for another night.

He closed the laptop and slid it back in his bag before sliding his bag under the low bed. If determined enough, someone could find his bag there, but he'd never had an issue with one soldier stealing from another on any previous deployment and he doubted he would now.

With the bag stowed, he changed out of his pants and into a more comfortable pair of shorts before climbing into the bed. He should brush his teeth but as the room didn't contain a bathroom, he didn't feel like getting dressed again just to brush his teeth and undress again. No, it could wait until morning, but then he would be sure to make a night brushing part of his routine. Routine, he thought, as his eyes closed. That's what he needed to do tomorrow. Figure out the routine.

23

HEIDI

"*B*ella, are you ready yet?" Heidi checked her watch again. It was seven in the morning, and Bella had yet to appear for breakfast. They would have to leave in forty minutes for Heidi to make it to work on time. "Bella?"

When there was no reply, Heidi sighed and dropped the knife she had just retrieved in order to make a sandwich for Bella for lunch. She walked to Bella's room and knocked on the door. "Bella, are you awake?"

"Go away," came the muffled voice from inside. "I'm not going to school today."

Heidi blew out a frustrated breath. She should have known Bella would fight her today. It had been the same thing yesterday as she tried to get the girl to go to church. She had refused to get out of bed, refused to get dressed, and finally Heidi had given in and watched the service online. However, that wasn't an option today. She had to get to work, and Bella had to go to school.

Pushing the door open, Heidi entered the room. "Bella, I know you are sad, but you cannot stay in bed all day today. It is Monday, and you have school this week. I have to get to work, and you have to get to school. Besides, you love school, remember?"

"I love my daddy," Bella mumbled from the bed. "Not school."

Heidi flicked on the light and crossed to the closet. She pulled out a pink shirt and then turned to the dresser and retrieved a pair of jeans and a pair of socks. "Do you want help getting dressed?" she asked as she placed the items on Bella's bed.

Bella looked up at her, her little face scrunched in sadness and frustration. "No, I can get dressed myself."

Heidi forced a smile. She knew Bella was hurting - she was too - but one could only wallow for so long. "I'll give you five minutes, and if you're not out by then, I'll be back to help you get dressed."

Bella sighed and pushed her blankets back. "I'm up and I can dress myself."

With that, Heidi patted Bella's leg, offered another smile, and headed back to the kitchen. She finished making the sandwiches for lunch, packed them, and started her waffle before the soft patter of feet entered the kitchen.

"Well, good morning," she said, smiling at Bella. The girl's hair needed a brushing, but at least she had managed to get herself dressed and in the room before the five minutes were up.

"Hmph," Bella said as she climbed up on a barstool. "Can I have cereal for breakfast?"

"Of course. Cocoa Puffs or Cinnamon Toast Crunch today?"

Bella sighed, sending her bangs lifting on her forehead for a moment. "Cocoa Puffs."

Heidi grabbed a bowl and filled it for Bella before rescuing her waffle from the maker and pulling up a chair beside the girl. "I know you miss your dad, but remember how much fun you have with Ms. Fields?"

Bella shrugged. "I guess, but it would be better if my dad were here."

"Everything is more fun with your dad here, but we have to learn to get on without him for a few months. What if we make him a video today?"

A tiny light flickered in Bella's eyes and she sat a little straighter. "A video? Like we can talk with him?"

"Well, we'll get to video chat with him tomorrow, but I was thinking a video of you telling him about your day. Then we can send it to him."

Bella's light dimmed. "I guess that would be okay. Not as fun as talking to him though."

"I know," Heidi said as she poured syrup on her waffle, "but tonight is when the families around here get together. That should be fun, right?"

Bella's shoulders lifted in a small shrug. "Yeah, I guess. Dad was always too busy to join them, but I've always wanted to."

"Then we will remedy that tonight. I think it will be a lot of fun, and a great end to the first day." Heidi sent another smile Bella's direction and was relieved when the corners of the girl's mouth lifted in return.

Half an hour later, they pulled into the parking lot of the school and Heidi pulled out her camera. "What do you want to say to Daddy?" she asked as she jumped over to the camera icon.

"I want to tell him that I miss him and that he should be here," Bella said.

Heidi hit pause on the video and winked at Bella. "Okay, done. Shall we go show him your classroom again?" Cory had managed to spare a little time to drop Bella off on her first day, so he'd seen the classroom, but it had been rushed and frenzied that morning and he hadn't been back since. This would allow Bella to give him a mini tour.

"Yeah, let's do it." She grabbed her bag and pushed open the door.

Heidi had her pause at the front door so that she could snap a picture in front of the school sign. Then they headed inside and to her kindergarten room. Linley met them at the door with a smile.

"Hello, Miss Bella," she said, bending down to smile at the girl. "How are you doing this morning?"

Heidi had been relieved when Bella had been assigned to Linley's classroom. She knew her friend would not only keep an eye on the girl, but would inform Heidi if there were any issues. If she couldn't be Bella's teacher, having Linley be was the next best thing.

"I'm okay," Bella said, "but I miss my dad."

"Do you mind if we record a quick video for her dad?" Heidi asked, holding up the camera and wiggling it.

"Not at all. Just try not to get any of the other students in the shot if they come in. For privacy reasons."

"Of course," Heidi said with a nod. She turned to Bella. "You ready?"

"What should I do?" the girl asked, looking excited for the first time in two days.

"How about you do a virtual tour and show Daddy what you do each day?"

Bella nodded and headed over to a shelving area that was labeled with names. Heidi began recording as Bella took off her backpack, unzipped it to grab her lamb, and then placed it in her correct cubby area.

"Hey, Daddy," she said, turning to Heidi, "this is

where I put my backpack each day. Look, it has my name." She pointed to the masking tape label with a wide smile. "And over there is the reading corner. It has lots of beanbags."

She moved to the beanbags and motioned to them like a tiny Vanna White. "I can't read on my own yet, but I'm getting better."

"I bet you'll be reading when Daddy gets home," Heidi said with a wink.

"That's a good goal. I'm going to learn to read before you get back then, Daddy," Bella said proudly at the camera.

"Okay," Heidi said, pushing the stop button, "I have to go greet my students too, but I'll get this put together for your dad, and I'm right down the hall if you need anything."

Bella's smile dropped slightly, but she nodded. "I can come to you if I need you?"

"Of course," Linley said, placing an arm around Bella, "but I'm here too."

"Okay."

Heidi pulled Bella in for a hug, flashed Linley a grateful smile, and then headed out to start her day.

24

CORY

$\mathcal{C}$ory smiled as he pulled up the videos of Bella that he had just received. He'd been fortunate enough to snag an open internet connection after his shift and had jumped on hoping he'd have news from home. He hadn't expected a video, but that had been waiting for him as he opened his email.

He clicked play and fought the tears that threatened to spill out of his eyes as he watched his daughter tell him how much she missed him and give him a small tour of her new classroom. He'd seen it briefly on the first day, but it was nice to see she knew her way around it now, and she looked beautiful. He wished he was there to tell her that in person. The video of Bella faded, and he was about to click the X in the corner to close it when Heidi's face popped up. The background behind her was different, so she must have recorded it at a different time.

"Hey, Cory. I hope you're doing well. Bella had a rough weekend, but making the video for you appeared to cheer her up slightly. We're meeting with some of your neighbors tonight, so I hope that will help too." She paused and nibbled on her bottom lip before sighing. "I don't know if I'm supposed to say this, but I miss you and not just because taking care of Bella would be easier with you here. I miss you. I wish-"

A bell sounded interrupting her, and her eyes darted away from the camera for a moment. She sighed. "Sorry, I have to go, but I look forward to talking with you tomorrow."

Cory closed the video after making sure there was nothing else and sat staring at the screen for a minute. Heidi's words tugged at his heart. She hadn't said she loved him - not in so many words - but he could see the emotion in her eyes. And if he were honest, he felt the same. Did he love her? He wasn't sure, but he definitely cared about her. Something had certainly shifted since their wedding and especially since their kiss.

He placed his fingers on the keys to respond to her email, but he didn't know what to say to her. He could tell her that he missed her too, but would that be enough?

"Hard finding the right words sometimes, isn't it?"

Cory looked to his right to see a fellow soldier at the

terminal next to him. "Yeah, sometimes it is." He didn't recognize the soldier but it didn't matter. Once soldiers deployed together, they were like brothers anyway.

"I remember writing letters to my wife was always the hardest," the guy said as he plugged his own laptop in. "I never knew how much to share as I didn't want to worry her."

Cory was familiar with that feeling. He'd never known how much to tell Desiree either. Nor did he know how much to tell Heidi, but that wasn't really his issue.

"Tell you what though, I wish I still had that to worry about."

"What do you mean?" Cory asked.

"My wife passed away a few months ago."

"I'm sorry to hear that man. My wife died a year ago, my first wife, I mean."

The man's brows lifted. "You married again, already?"

Heat rushed across Cory's face. "I had to. I have a daughter and no one to take care of her, but I didn't marry a stranger. She was my best friend in high school."

The man nodded as if he understood. And he probably did. The military was like that. Because they endured things that most people didn't have to, they understood a lot that others didn't have to as well. "That's cool and understandable, but if you don't mind me asking, why do you look like you're having such trouble writing to a woman who was your best friend in high school?"

Cory sighed. "I asked her to marry me because we were friends, and I thought if we could stay that way then I wouldn't be going against my vows to my first wife, but somewhere along the way, I think I developed feelings for Heidi. Now, I'm not sure what to say." He leaned back and scraped his hand across his chin. "Neither of us declared our feelings before I left, but I was fairly certain she felt something. Then I got this email, and now I don't know what to say back."

The man next to him smiled. "I know it's hard to open your heart again, but I'd bet money that your first wife wouldn't want you to be unhappy. She'd want you to keep on living and if that meant finding love again, I think she'd be supportive of that."

"Yeah, I guess in my head I know that. We even had conversations about that though it was usually me telling her to find someone else if something happened to me, but it's hard to tell my heart, you know?"

"I do," the man said with a nod. "The heart is a tricky thing, but there is someone you can always talk to about matters of the heart."

"I don't really feel like sharing all this with a chaplain," Cory said with a soft snort. "I'm not even sure why I'm telling you all of this."

The man's smile widened. "I get that a lot, but I wasn't talking about a chaplain. I was talking about Jesus. I never knew what a good listener He was until my wife died, but now I feel empty if a day goes by where I don't talk to Him."

Cory bit the inside of his lip as he processed the man's words. Jesus. He sure had been coming up a lot lately in Cory's life, and if he was honest, he had felt more peace after reading the Bible the other day. Maybe it was time to take his concerns to God and let Him be in control for once. "Thanks, I'll think about it."

"He'll always be there when you're ready." With that the man pushed back from his chair and stood.

"Weren't you going to use the computer?" Cory asked.

The man smiled. "Nah, I'm good. I accomplished what I came here to do." He placed a hand on Cory's shoulder before walking away.

Cory watched the man exit the tent. What had that been about? Shaking his head, he turned back to the computer. He needed to respond to Heidi, but more than that, he needed to figure out how he felt and what to do about it.

He thought back to the verse he'd read yesterday. Maybe it was time to let God lead his life again. Closing his eyes, he sent a prayer heavenward.

"God," he whispered softly, "I know it's been a while, but I need you in my life again. I need you to lead me and help me be a good husband to Heidi and a good father to Bella. Please help me figure out how to tell her how I feel and keep us all safe until I can return home and tell her in person." He paused for a moment, unsure of what else to say. "Thanks for listening. Amen."

It hadn't been the most eloquent prayer, but it had worked, and as Cory put his fingers back on the keys, an idea began to form in his head.

25

HEIDI

"*B*ella? Are you ready? It's almost time to Skype with Daddy." Heidi opened the laptop and jumped to the Skype app to get it loaded.

"Yes!" Bella's exuberant reply came just shortly before she appeared around the corner like a whirlwind. Her hair flew behind her as her little legs and arms pumped.

"No need to run," Heidi said with a smile. "He's not even here yet."

"But I don't want to miss a thing," Bella said as she slowed down and then climbed onto the chair.

A moment later, the doorbell chime sounded, and the screen jumped as Cory's face filled the view.

"Daddy," Bella hollered. She leaned close to the screen as if intending to plant a kiss on his picture.

Heidi touched her shoulder. "He can't see you when you get that close, Bella."

Bella leaned back, and Cory's smiling face appeared once again. "Hey, pumpkin. How are you?"

"I'm okay, Daddy, but I miss you."

"I miss you too, bug. How is school?"

Bella grinned and bobbed her head. "It's good. Ms. Fields is nice and pretty, but not as pretty as Ms. Heidi." She turned to Heidi and flashed a cheesy smile as if she knew she was flattering her.

Cory chuckled. "That's good. What else do you like about school?"

"Um." Bella pursed her lips and tapped them with her index finger. "We get three recesses."

"Three? That is lucky. I don't remember ever getting three. Did you ever get three recesses, Heidi?"

Heidi leaned down so that she would be in the camera frame as well. "I think we only had one, but it has been a while since I was young enough to have recess."

"Me too." As Cory smiled, an odd sensation stole over Heidi. His smile was different today. More genuine or easier or something.

"So what else have you been doing, bug?" Cory asked, shifting the conversation.

"Well, last night we went across the street and had pizza and played games with the neighbors. We should have done that sooner, Daddy. It was so much fun."

"You're right. We should have, but I promise you we will continue to hang out with them when I get back. How's that?"

Bella nodded vigorously. "That would be awesome. The girl, I think her name is Ella, she has so many dolls. I got to play with some of them. Maybe we can get more dolls?"

"I'll tell you what," Cory said with a smile, "when I get back, we'll go doll shopping and you can pick two new dolls."

"Yes. That would be awesome. Can Ms. Heidi get something new too?"

"If she wants." Cory held Heidi's gaze for a moment and again she felt that something was different. She hoped she would get a chance to ask him what.

As Cory and Bella continued to chat, Heidi slipped away to begin preparing dinner. She pulled ingredients from the pantry and listened to them chat back and forth. As she did, she wondered if she and Cory would ever have that rapport again. They had once been like that in high school, thick as thieves, but the kiss at the wedding had changed everything. Heidi had long had romantic feelings for him, but now she was beginning to believe she might be in love with him which would be wonderful except for the fact that she didn't think he felt the same way.

Stifling a small sigh, she sent up a prayer. She'd

thought often about how she would feel in a marriage not based on love, but she had never considered she might end up in a marriage of unrequited love.

"Miss Heidi."

Heidi harnessed her wandering thoughts and turned to Bella. "Is something wrong?"

"No, but Daddy says he has to go soon and he wanted to talk to you."

"Oh, okay." Heidi returned to the table, curious as to what Cory would need to say to her. It probably had something to do with Bella or perhaps some important detail he had forgotten to tell her.

"Bye Daddy," Bella said before racing from the room and leaving the chair open for Heidi.

"Hi," Heidi said as she took the still warm seat. She could not believe how utterly self-conscious she felt around Cory now.

"Hey." He seemed just as nervous as she did which made her feel a little better. "How are you doing?"

"I'm okay. It's been busy at school. Bella was sad this weekend, but starting school again has seemed to help."

"That's good. That's good." His eyes shifted from her to the floor and back again as he chewed on his lip. She had never seen him so nervous. "I read your email, and I wanted to tell you that I miss you too."

"Oh, that's nice to hear." Heidi wasn't sure what else

to say. She appreciated the fact that he missed her, but that was all? She was sure he missed his parents and his bed. He probably even missed his car. That didn't make her feel special in the least.

Cory sighed and rubbed his chin. "I'm sorry, that didn't come out right. I do miss you, but I wanted to tell you that I'm sorry."

"For what?"

"I should have told you that night after the wedding or the day after, but I was scared. I felt like if I felt something for you, then I was dishonoring my late wife, but I do, Heidi. I feel more for you than friendship. That kiss. I just..."

Heidi smiled as he stumbled over the words. She wished he was here so that she could have one of those movie moments where she could stop his fumbling with a kiss and tell him she loved him too, but that would have to wait. "I love you too, Cory. I think I kind of always have, but I knew it when you kissed me."

Relief flooded Cory's face. "You do?"

"I do."

He chuckled and then sighed. "I'm sorry I didn't kiss you again. I wish I could be there now to do it."

"Me too, but just knowing you want to is good for now."

For a moment they stared at each other and then a warning bell sounded. Cory's face fell. "Ugh, that's my warning. I have to get off, but I'll call you again this weekend?"

"We'll be here," Heidi said. She knew the next six months would be challenging, but now that she knew how Cory felt, she also knew that she could make it until he returned.

SIX MONTHS LATER - CORY

*C*ory wished he'd had the chance to shower more recently as he grabbed his bag and headed for the plane's exit. While he was sure Heidi and Bella would understand, he still wished he could wash the stale airplane funk off him before seeing them. However, that hadn't been an option.

The bright light of the sun hit him as he stepped off the plane. Though it was only early March, the air was relatively warm and much different than the interior of the plane. He lifted his free hand to shield his eyes. As he did, he heard Bella's sweet voice call his name.

"Daddy."

She appeared a moment later, bursting through the small crowd and racing at full speed toward him. In preparation, he dropped his bag and held out his arms. He had no idea how she had seen him before he'd seen her, but he was ready to hug her now. She jumped into his arms with such force that he had to take a step back to maintain his balance.

"Hey, bug. I've missed you." He squeezed her tight, enjoying the smell of her hair and the joy of hugging his little girl again.

"I've missed you too, Daddy. I'm so glad you're home."

Cory planted a kiss on her cheek then scanned the area behind her for Heidi. As the crowd shifted again, he saw her watching them both. Her auburn hair blew softly in the wind like tiny copper kite tails. When their eyes met, the corners of her lips curled up in a smile before she began walking toward them.

"Hey," she said when she reached them.

Cory could have responded with words, but none seemed important enough to utter. Instead, he circled her waist with his free hand and pulled her in for a kiss. She hesitated for only a moment before wrapping one arm around his neck and one arm around Bella, who was still clinging to him on the other side.

The kiss was everything he had imagined for the last six months and more. Even the sound of Bella yelling and clapping in his other ear didn't distract him from enjoying the taste of Heidi's lips and the feel of her in his arms. He'd dreamed of this moment every day for the last six months but his dreams didn't even come close to the real thing.

"I'm glad you're back," Heidi said when the kiss ended.

"Not back," Cory said. "Home. Let's go home."

SIXTEEN MONTHS Later - Heidi

Heidi stared down at the bundle in her arms and examined every inch. Baby Benjamin looked a lot like Cory, at least right now. His eyes were currently closed, but his nose was the same, and he even had a tiny cleft in his chin just like his daddy.

"You did great, Heidi," Cory said, smoothing her hair back from her eyes.

Heidi smiled up at him, but she felt like she'd had it pretty easy. From the day she found out she was pregnant, she'd been excited but also a little nervous about the delivery. While she loved the new friends she'd made on post, they'd shared their scary delivery stories when they found out she was pregnant which had only increased her nervousness about the pain and the recovery.

However, when her water had broken this morning, she'd been eerily calm.

"Cory, I think you'll need to call in today," she hollered from the bathroom.

"Why?" His voice was still heavy with sleep.

"Because my water just broke." This was Heidi's first pregnancy, but she'd thought she would feel something when her water broke - massive pain, contractions, something, but other than the extra gush of water she felt nothing.

"What?" Cory bolted out of bed and rushed to her side, placing his hand on her belly. *"Are you sure?"*

"Well, pretty sure."

"Are you having contractions?"

Heidi shook her head. *"I don't think so. I don't have any pain. Maybe they come later?"*

Cory ran his hand down his face. *"I don't remember. It's been so long. Okay, what do we need to do?"* His eyes darted around the room as if searching for a hint there.

Heidi placed a hand on his arm. *"The first thing we need to do is not freak out. Call work. I'll call Linley. We'll drop Bella off with her and then head to the hospital."*

"Right," Cory said with a nod, *"that's a good plan."*

Heidi smiled as she thought back over the morning. It had definitely been one to remember. After dropping Bella off, they had checked into the hospital where the doctor confirmed her water had broken. The contractions didn't follow though, so after three hours of waiting, the doctor had recommended Pitocin to speed up the labor. Heidi consented, and an hour later, the pain had finally hit.

When the nurse offered an epidural, Heidi had agreed, and after the uncomfortable procedure, the pain had subsided. However, when the doctor returned half an hour later for a check up, she announced that Heidi's labor had started. Heidi had felt nothing, and the doctor had been forced to tell her when to push as she couldn't feel the contractions.

Though she knew she would be sore when the drug finally wore off, Heidi couldn't help thinking that she'd kind of cheated. Her delivery had been nothing like the movies - no sweaty, exhausted woman cursing at her husband for putting her in the current situation, no crying in pain, just pushing when the doctor said to and then hearing her son cry when he entered the world.

"We did great," she said, smiling up at Cory.

'Knock knock," a soft voice called from the doorway, "can we come in?"

Heidi looked over to see Linley poking her head in the doorway which meant that Bella had to be close behind. Cory must have called or texted her as soon as Benjamin was born.

"Of course," Heidi said. She couldn't wait to show Bella her baby brother.

When Heidi and Cory had first announced the news, Bella had been happy. She'd rattled on non-stop about how great it would be to have a sister to play with, and even though Cory and Heidi had tried to tell her it might be a boy, she'd been convinced the baby would be a girl.

When the ultrasound revealed the baby was a boy, Bella had lost her enthusiasm for a time, but once they began turning Heidi's old room into a nursery, her excitement had been renewed. From that moment on, she'd been determined to be the best big sister ever - even if it was to a boy.

Linley pushed the door open, and Bella entered like a streak of lightning. In a flash, she was at Heidi's bedside.

"Can I see him now? Can I?" she asked, bouncing on her toes.

"Of course you can," Cory said with a laugh. Though she was growing like a weed, Cory was still strong enough to hoist Bella up in his arms, and as he did, Heidi turned the bundle toward Bella.

"Aw, he's so cute," Bella said, her voice taking on a higher tone than normal. "Will I get to hold him?"

"When we get home and you're sitting down," Heidi said with a smile. "I promise I'll teach you how to take care of him, and I'll let you help as much as you want."

Heidi expected Bella to react with a cheer or a grin, but instead a serious expression stole across her face.

"What's the matter?" Heidi asked as the little girl's eyes filled with tears.

"Now that Benjamin's here and he's your real baby, does that mean you won't love me as much?"

Heidi's heart broke at the soft words. She should have realized this thought might cross Bella's mind, but she hadn't.

"Come here," she said, patting the bed beside her after

handing Benjamin to Linley. "I might not be the mother who brought you into this world, but you will always be my daughter, Bella, and no matter how many kids we have, that will never change. And I will never love you less."

Bella sniffed and looked up at her with big eyes. "You promise?"

"I promise," Heidi said.

Cory took Benjamin from Linley and stepped closer to the bed. "I promise too. We're so grateful to have Benjamin in our family, but nothing and no one will ever replace you," he said.

Bella's eyes shifted to Cory and the baby in his arms. "So, we'll always be family?"

Heidi smiled as she caught Cory's gaze. Their relationship might not have started in the usual way, but she had no doubt they would make it last. After all, she'd married her best friend, and their love had only deepened since his return. She didn't know what the future held, but she knew they could face anything together.

"Always," Heidi said. "We'll always be family."

Bella's face remained serious a moment longer before she finally shrugged and said, "I guess we can keep him then."

As the room filled with laughter, Heidi looked to the ceiling and sent a prayer of thanks to God. He'd proven to her once again that He would take care of everything if she would just trust Him. And it had turned out better than she ever could have imagined.

The End!

If you enjoyed this book, would you leave a review? It really helps!

AUTHOR'S NOTE

~

First off, let me say how glad I am that you read this book. When my friend Evangeline Kelly and I brainstormed this bride idea, I had no idea what I was going to write at first. Then The Cowboy's Reality Bride came to me. I created so many wonderful characters in that book that I knew some of them would need their own story, so I continued the series with The Producer's Unlikely Bride.

I always knew Heidi had a story, but I have to tell you that this one was the hardest. 2020 was a hard year with all the lockdowns. Then, due to a teacher deciding not to return, I was asked to take on two more sections than I had planned. That severely cut down my writing time.

Then the election happened and my heart was heavy for a long time.

I'm trying to turn it all to God, and thankfully, I got a few good weeks where I pounded this out. Even though it was a challenge for me to get through, I hope you enjoyed it.

And if you've enjoyed reading this author's note so far (and really, how could you not?) I am offering, for today only, a page where you can sign up for my weekly newsletter for the low, low price of absolutely nothing.

Included in this weekly newsletter are many wonderful things like pictures of my adorable children, chances to win awesome prizes, new releases and sales I might be holding, great books from other authors, and anything else that strikes my fancy and that I think you would enjoy.

Even better, I solemnly swear to only send out one newsletter a week (usually on Tuesday unless life gets in the way which with three kids it usually does). I will not spam you, sell your email address to solicitors or anyone else, or any of those other terrible things.

Join me here and receive a free novella as my thank-you gift for choosing to hang out with me. It's fun and entertaining. I promise.

Prayers and blessings,

Lorana

NOT READY TO SAY GOODBYE YET?

The Producer's Unlikely Bride is the sixth book in the multi-author Blushing Bride series, but my second (or third if you count the bonus short story, The Reality Bride's Baby). While each book written by a different author in the series will be a stand alone, I have decided to make mine a series. If you are reading on Amazon, the numbers may look confusing, but just know that my books will twine together. You don't have to have read The Cowboy's Reality Bride for this book to make sense, but if you have, you will have a better understanding of Justin and Peter.

I have loved writing about brides, but they haven't done as well as I'd hoped. With that in mind, I am taking Cassidy, one of the hopeful daters, from The Cowboy's Reality Bride and starting a spin-off series called The Men of Fire Beach. This will combine firefighters, doctors, and cops. The new title will be Flames of Attraction

The book will open after Cassidy returns home from being on the show. Obviously she didn't find love, but what she has found is a ton of guys trying to court her and massive teasing from her fellow firefighters.

Fire Games

A firefighter who just wants to get back to work.

Cassidy is glad to be back home after the reality dating

show, but she did not expect to return to a bag of fan mail complete with obsessive letters. The cop assigned to help her doesn't seem too concerned, but when she sees something at a fire that makes no sense, will she be able to convince him to take her seriously?

He's a cop who's avoided Cassidy as much as possible.

But not because he doesn't like her. Unfortunately Cassidy reminds Jordan of a painful past. However, when she sees something odd during a fire, he is forced to spend time with her to figure out what it all means

Turn the page for a sneak peek

A LOOK AT A NEW SERIES

Chapter 1

Cassidy Marcel gazed at the firehouse with trepidation. She loved her job, but she also knew firefighters. They loved to razz each other over everything, and her appearance on the reality dating show, Who Wants to Marry a Cowboy, would be no exception. Plus, she wondered how Captain Fitzgerald was going to react. The stony-faced Captain hadn't been her biggest fan before she took three weeks off; she assumed she would be even lower on his list now.

Inhaling deeply, she pulled her shoulders back hoping she appeared more confident than she felt. Then she opened her car door, tucked her dark hair behind her ears, and walked into the lion's den.

"Marcel, so glad you could grace us with your presence again." Billy Campbell, or Bubba, as everyone called him stood before her, a giant smile on his face. He was one of her favorite people in the firehouse. Originally from Texas, he had a heart bigger than his smile and was more like an older brother than a co-worker. "I didn't want you to feel like we didn't want you, so I thought this my help." From behind his back, he brandished a miniature black cowboy hat and held it out to her. Though small, it somehow sported sequins that caught and shimmered in the light.

Cassidy rolled her eyes good naturedly as she shook her head. She should have expected something like this, especially after the sugar incident last year. Sugar wouldn't have to grace her grocery list for another six months at least. "Haha, thanks, Bubba. I missed you too." She grabbed the hat knowing several more of these would be in store before the day was through. "Did I miss any excitement while I was gone?"

Bubba pushed open the door to the common room that doubled as a living room and the kitchen area. "Only if you count Luca's boycott of Deacon's Paleo meal plan."

"It's not a meal if there's no potatoes in it," Luca said speaking up from the couch. Luca was a Southern boy as well, and he believed every meal should include meat and potatoes. And chocolate. The man insisted that every meal come with a dessert which explained the extra twenty pounds he carried on his frame. Somehow though it didn't hinder him in his job. He was strong and agile and quicker than almost all of them. His eyes flicked up briefly from the television he was watching. "Oh, hey, Marcel, welcome back." He launched something at her without ever taking his eyes off the screen.

She knew what it was before it landed a few inches from her. Another miniature cowboy hat. This one was brown and had a tiny feather. Cassidy picked it up and flashed Luca a crooked grin. "Thanks, Luca. I missed you too."

"Forgive him. He didn't like the brownies I gave him with dinner last night, and he's still sour about it," Deacon said as he stepped around the island in the kitchen and toward her and Bubba. Strong and dark skinned, Deacon was the epitome of an oxymoron. His bulging muscles gave him an intimidating presence, but inside he was the biggest teddy bear. He pulled her in for a hug before brandishing his own miniature hat.

Cassidy chuckled as she took the hat though she had no idea what she was going to do with all of these. She had only kept one from the show and that was more as a souvenir than anything else. And a reminder to never do something like that again.

"Brownies don't have prunes in them," Luca spoke up from the couch.

Cassidy lifted a brow at Deacon. "You made brownies

with prunes? Things really have changed in a month." It wasn't that prunes were completely out of the norm for Deacon. He regarded his body as a temple and rarely put anything processed in it, but he also wasn't one for sweets generally. He focused more on macronutrients and desserts rarely fit in his plan.

Deacon shrugged. "I thought I could slip some healthy desserts in on these guys. Keep them a little trimmer in the middle if you know what I mean." He patted his rock-hard abs.

"Might have worked too, if you hadn't eaten them as well," Bubba said with a deep laugh. "That was clue number one they had to be healthy. You really couldn't taste the prunes though, but man did they wreak havoc on my insides later."

"Okay, enough of that," Cassidy said shaking her head and squeezing her eyes shut. The image of a run on the bathroom was not the visual she wanted to have of her fellow firemen.

"Cassidy, oh my gosh, I'm so glad you're back."

Cassidy would have recognized Ivy's voice anywhere. Not only was she the only other woman in the firehouse, but her voice held just the slightest valley girl twang. On anyone else it might have been annoying, but Ivy was wholesomely sweet, down to earth, and as cute as a button. Her blond hair perfectly framed her heart-shaped face, and big blue eyes sat above a ski-sloped nose that contained no trace of freckles, unlike Cassidy's.

Ivy attacked her with a hug before Cassidy was ready and the gesture jostled her full arms sending the contents flying to the floor. Ivy's eyes widened as she released Cassidy and her petite hand flew to her mouth. "I'm so sorry. I was just so excited to see you. You don't know how awful it's been being the only woman here for the last month." She dropped to the floor to help Cassidy pick up the hats.

Ivy was teasing mostly, but Cassidy had been at the firehouse before Ivy arrived, and she remembered how hard it was being the only female. "Don't worry about it. They're just silly hats, and I'm sorry I left you high and dry."

"Marcel? Is that you?"

Cassidy froze at the stern sound of her captain's voice. Having been recently promoted, Captain Darryl Fitzgerald was now all business. Every rule needed to be followed to the letter and the teasing shut down when he was around. She snatched the hat and stood. "Good morning, Captain, what can I do for you?"

"You can follow me to my office. We need to have a chat."

"Of course, sir." Cassidy fought the anxiety clawing at her throat. Captain Fitzgerald was intimidating, but she had just returned. She couldn't have done anything too bad. Maybe it was about the hats. She would explain that the guys were just razzing her a little and then take them to her car so they were out of sight.

Cassidy's anxiety increased when Captain Fitzgerald shut the door to his office behind her. Closed door meetings rarely held a good outcome. "Have I done something, sir?" She hated the slight tremble in her voice, but she knew he controlled her future and she loved her job.

"Sit." He pointed at one of the chairs opposite his desk and then walked to his own chair and sat down. "I know that you had time saved up for this trip, but I need someone I can rely on in this firehouse."

"I understand, sir, and I have no intention of going anywhere else anytime soon."

He leaned back in his chair and folded his arms across his chest. "That is good to hear, but to be sure, I am placing you back on probation. You'll have cleaning duty for the next month, and I want that truck sparkling at the end of every shift. Is that clear?"

Cassidy had no idea if he had the power to do that since she technically had done nothing wrong, but she wasn't going to argue with him. She loved this job and this house. No way did she want to go back to being a floater, so if he wanted her to wash the truck every day, she would do it. If he wanted to put her on kitchen duty, she would do that too even though her cooking left a lot to be desired. "Crystal clear, sir. I promise I am committed to this job and will do whatever it takes to prove it to you."

"Perfect, now we should discuss the mail situation." He steepled his fingers and regarded her with a cool stare.

She furrowed her brow, confused as to what he could mean. "I'm sorry, the what?"

His eyebrow inched up his forehead. "You don't know?" Cassidy shook her head. "It appears you garnered a few fans while you were gallivanting on your show, and as they didn't know where you lived, they dropped your mail here."

Cassidy winced and bit the inside of her lip. No wonder he was angry. "I had no idea, sir. I'm so sorry."

He waved a hand dismissing her. "It is what it is, but I want them gone from the firehouse at the end of your shift."

"Of course sir. Um, where are they?"

He nodded to the corner of the room. Cassidy turned and spied a large brown bag that she hadn't noticed when they entered. Roughly the size of a burlap sack, it bulged and protruded as wide as appeared possible. "All of that is for me?"

"Yep, letters, gifts, you name it. I suggest you find a better place for it."

"Yes sir." Cassidy pulled her shoulders back as she faced the mountainous bag. Since shift had just started, she might as well drag it to the bunk room and go through it while there was time. She didn't need all of this cluttering her small house either.

The bag proved unwieldy but thankfully just enough extra sack remained at the top that she was able to drag it down the hallway and into the bunk room. Meant generally for sleeping when they worked long shifts, the bunk room held rows and rows of two beds separated by half walls. A small table that held a lamp sat between each two-bed section.

She and Ivy shared the section at the very back of the room, and sweat rolled down Cassidy's spine as she dragged the bag to the bunk she normally slept in. With a sigh and an exhalation, she plopped down on the bunk and opened the bag. If Santa had been real, she would know exactly how he felt. She grabbed one of the envelopes and opened it.

"Dear Cassidy, I saw you on the show, and I think we'd make a great couple. I love horses and roller skating. You can call me at 555-1324. Signed, David. P.S. If a woman answers, it's just my mom."

Cassidy shook her head and laid the letter to the side. No need to keep that one. She wanted a man established enough that he lived on his own or maybe with a roommate. Rent wasn't cheap in the city, but moms were a no go. With a sigh, she reached into the bag again. It was going to be a long afternoon.

**

Jordan issued his apology as he hurried into the office. "Sorry I'm late. We were helping with a drug bust."

"Of course you were," Graham said with a roll of his eyes.

"It's no problem, Jordan, we were just getting started." Mr. Keyes, their father's attorney adjusted his tie before placing his hands on either side of a stack of papers. "I'm sure you know that I called you in today for a reading of your father's will. Most of it is rather straightforward, but there is something I wasn't sure you were aware of." He picked up the top sheet of paper and scanned it before flipping it around to them. "Did you know your father owned a bar?"

"A bar?" Graham asked leaning forward.

"That's not possible. Dad was an alcoholic. Why would he own a bar?" Jordan asked.

"It hasn't been a bar in a long time. I drove by the other day, so I would have current information for you both. It appears to be boarded up currently." He pulled a picture from the stack and slid it across the table to Graham who glanced at it before handing it to Jordan.

"So, we should just try and sell it, right?" Jordan asked. He had no use for a bar or the rundown building in the picture.

"No, we can't sell it. Dad obviously kept the bar for a reason," Graham said.

"He probably just forgot he owned it and therefore

forgot to sell it. What would we do with an old building?"

Mr. Keyes said nothing but moved his head from one brother to the next as they argued.

"What would we do?" Graham turned in his chair to face Jordan. "We fix it up, give it new life, take it back to how it once was."

Jordan shook his head. "I have no time to fix up a bar. And what about the money? Did Dad leave any money to fix this bar?"

"Your father left you the proceeds from the sale of the house and he had a few stocks and bonds, but it isn't much."

"See? It isn't much. Probably not enough to fix up an old bar."

Graham folded his arms across his chest. "I'm not selling. Dad could have sold the building years ago, and he didn't. That tells me it meant something to him, so I'm going to restore it with or without you."

Jordan turned fierce eyes on the lawyer. "Can he do that? Can he make me keep it?"

Mr. Keyes shrugged. "He could offer to buy you out, but there is no stipulation that he has to sell."

Before he could say anything else, Jordan's phone buzzed. He swiped the screen, shook his head, and stood. "I have to go, but this isn't over. We are going to discuss this Graham."

Click here to order your copy today!

A FREE STORY FOR YOU!

Enjoyed this story? Not ready to quit reading yet? If you sign up for my newsletter, you will receive The Billionaire's Impromptu Bet right away as my thank you gift for choosing to hang out with me.

A SWAT officer. A bored billionaire heiress. A bet that could change everything....

Read on for a taste of The Billionaire's Impromptu Bet....

THE BILLIONAIRE'S IMPROMPTU BET
PREVIEW

Brie Carter fell back spread eagle on her queen-sized canopy bed sending her blonde hair fanning out behind her. With a large sigh, she uttered, "I'm bored."

"How can you be bored? You have like millions of dollars." Her friend, Ariel, plopped down in a seated position on the bed beside her and flicked her raven hair off her shoulder. "You want to go shopping? I hear Tiffany's is having a special right now."

Brie rolled her eyes. Shopping? Where was the excitement in that? With her three platinum cards, she could go shopping whenever she wanted. "No, I'm bored with shopping too. I have everything. I want to do something exciting. Something we don't normally do."

Brie enjoyed being rich. She loved the unlimited credit cards at her disposal, the constant apparel of new clothes, and of course the penthouse apartment her father paid for, but lately, she longed for something more fulfilling.

Ariel's hazel eyes widened. "I know. There's a new bar down on Franklin Street. Why don't we go play a little game?"

Brie sat up, intrigued at the secrecy and the twinkle in Ariel's eyes. "What kind of game?"

"A betting game. You let me pick out any man in the place. Then you try to get him to propose to you."

Brie wrinkled her nose. "But I don't want to get married." She loved her freedom and didn't want to share her penthouse with anyone, especially some man.

"You don't marry him, silly. You just get him to propose."

Brie bit her lip as she thought. It had been awhile since her last relationship and having a man dote on her for a month might be interesting, but.... "I don't know. It doesn't seem very nice."

"How about I sweeten the pot? If you win, I'll set you up on a date with my brother."

Brie cocked her head. Was she serious? The only thing Brie couldn't seem to buy in the world was the affection of Ariel's very handsome, very wealthy, brother. He was a movie star, just the kind of person Brie could consider marrying in the future. She'd had a crush on him as long as she and Ariel had been friends, but he'd always seen her as just that, his little sister's friend. "I thought you didn't want me dating your brother."

"I don't." Ariel shrugged. "But he's between girlfriends right now, and I know you've wanted it for ages. If you win this bet, I'll set you up. I can't guarantee any more than one date though. The rest will be up to you."

Brie wasn't worried about that. Charm she possessed in abundance. She simply needed some alone time with him, and she was certain she'd be able to convince him they were meant to be together. "All right. You've got a deal."

Ariel smiled. "Perfect. Let's get you changed then and see who the lucky man will be.

A tiny tug pulled on Brie's heart that this still wasn't right, but she dismissed it. This was simply a means to an end, and he'd never have to know.

Jesse Calhoun relaxed as the rhythmic thudding of the speed bag reached his ears. Though he loved his job, it was stressful being the SWAT sniper. He hated having to take human lives and today had been especially rough. The team had been called out to a drug bust, and Jesse was forced to return fire at three hostiles. He didn't care that they fired at his team and himself first. Taking a life was always hard, and every one of them haunted his dreams.

"You gonna bust that one too?" His co-worker Brendan appeared by his side. Brendan was the opposite of Jesse in nearly every way. Where Jesse's hair was a dark copper, Brendan's was nearly black. Jesse sported paler skin and a dusting of freckles across his nose, but Brendan's skin was naturally dark and freckle free.

Jesse flashed a crooked grin, but kept his eyes on the small, swinging black bag. The speed bag was his way to release, but a few times he had started hitting while still too keyed up and he had ruptured the bag. Okay, five times, but who was counting really? Besides, it was a better way to calm his nerves than other things he could choose. Drinking, fights, gambling, women.

"Nah, I think this one will last a little longer." His shoulders began to burn, and he gave the bag another few punches for good measure before dropping his arms and letting it swing to a stop. "See? It lives to be hit at least another day." Every once in a while, Jesse missed training the way he used to. Before he joined the force, he had been an amateur boxer, on his way to being a pro, but a shoulder injury had delayed his training and forced him to consider something else. It had eventually healed, but by then he had lost his edge.

"Hey, why don't you come drink with us?" Brendan

clapped a hand on Jesse's shoulder as they headed into the locker room.

"You know I don't drink." Jesse often felt like the outsider of the team. While half of the six-man team was married, the other half found solace in empty bottles and meaningless relationships. Jesse understood that - their job was such that they never knew if they would come home night after night - but he still couldn't partake.

Brendan opened his locker and pulled out a clean shirt. He peeled off his current one and added deodorant before tugging on the new one. "You don't have to drink. Look, I won't drink either. Just come and hang out with us. You have no one waiting for you at home."

That wasn't entirely true. Jesse had Bugsy, his Boston Terrier, but he understood Brendan's point. Most days, Jesse went home, fed Bugsy, made dinner, and fell asleep watching TV on the couch. It wasn't much of a life. "All right, I'll go, but I'm not drinking."

Brendan's lips pulled back to reveal his perfectly white teeth. He bragged about them, but Jesse knew they were veneers. "That's the spirit. Hurry up and change. We don't want to leave the rest of the team waiting."

"Is everyone coming?" Jesse pulled out his shower necessities. Brendan might feel comfortable going out with just a new application of deodorant, but Jesse needed to wash more than just dirt and sweat off. He needed to wash the sound of the bullets and the sight of lifeless bodies from his mind.

"Yeah, Pat's wife is pregnant again and demanding some crazy food concoctions. Pat agreed to pick them up if she let him have an hour. Cam and Jared's wives are having a girls' night, so the whole gang can be together. It will be nice to hang out when we aren't worried about being shot at."

"Fine. Give me ten minutes. Unlike you, I like to clean up before I go out."

Brendan smirked. "I've never had any complaints. Besides, do you know how long it takes me to get my hair like this?"

Jesse shook his head as he walked into the shower, but he knew it was true. Brendan had rugged good looks and muscles to match. He rarely had a hard time finding a woman. Jesse on the other hand hadn't dated anyone in the last few months. It wasn't that he hadn't been looking, but he was quieter than his teammates. And he wasn't looking for right now. He was looking for forever. He just hadn't found it yet.

Click here to continue reading The Billionaire's Impromptu Bet.

THE STORY DOESN'T END!

You've met a few people and fallen in love....

I bet you're wondering how you can meet everyone else.

Star Lake Series:

Sealed with a Kiss: Meet the quirky cast of Star Lake and find out if Max and Layla will ever find love.

When Love Returns: Return to Star Lake to hear Presley's story and find out if she gets the second chance with her first love.

Once Upon a Star: Continue the journey when aspiring actress Audrey returns home with a baby. Will Blake finally get the nerve to share his feelings with her?

Love Conquers All: Meet Lanie Perkins Hall who never imagined being divorced at thirty or falling for an old friend, but will his secrets keep them apart?

The Star Lake Collection: Get the latter three stories in one place. Series will include book 1 when it releases around November 2020.

The Heartbeats Series:

Where It All Began: Sandra Baker finds forgiveness and healing even after making a horrible choice.

The Power of Prayer: Will Callie Green find true love or be defined by her mistake?

When Hearts Collide: When Amanda Adams goes to college, she finds a world she was not ready for. But will she also find true love?

A Past Forgiven: Jess Peterson has lived a life of abuse and lost her self worth, but when she finds herself pregnant, will she find new hope?

The Heartbeats Collection: Grab all four Heartbeats novels in one collection

Sweet Billionaires Series:

The Billionaire's Impromptu Bet: Can a spoiled rich girl change when a bet turns to love?

The Billionaire's Secret: Can a playboy settle down when he finds out he has a daughter who needs him?

A Brush with a Billionaire: What happens when a stuck up actor lands in a small town and needs help from a female mechanic?

The Billionaire's Christmas Miracle: A twist on

a Cinderella story when a billionaire meets a woman who doesn't belong at the ball.

The Billionaire's Cowboy Groom: Will one night six years ago keep Carrie from finding true love?

The Cowboy Billionaire: He's there for her land, but he never expected to fall for her.

The Billionaire's Bliss: This collection contains The Billionaire's Secret, The Billionaire's Christmas Miracle, and The Billionaire's Cowboy Groom

The Lawkeeper Series:

Lawfully Matched: When the man she agreed to marry turns out to have a dark past, will Kate have to return home or will she find love with her rescuer in this historical fiction?

Lawfully Justified: Can a bounty hunter and a widow find love together in this historical fiction?

The Scarlet Wedding: William and Emma are planning their wedding, but an outbreak and a return from his past force them to change their plans. Is a happily ever after still in their future in this historical fiction?

Lawfully Redeemed: What happens when a K9 cop falls for the brother of her suspect? Contemporary romance.

The Lawkeeper Collection: Get all four books in one collection

The Are You Listening Series:

The Still Small Voice: Will Jordan listen to God's prompting in this speculative fiction?

A Spark in the Darkness Will Jordan be able to help Raven before the rapture occurs?

The Beginning of the End: After the rapture, Raven is faced with reaching new believers and surviving a pandemic sent to destroy them all.

Faith over Fear coming soon: Forced into hiding, will Rave and the others make it to the end?

Blushing Brides Series:

The Cowboy's Reality Bride: He's agreed to be the bachelor on a reality dating show, but what happens when he falls for a woman who's not one of the contestants?

The Reality Bride's Baby: Laney wants nothing more than a baby, but when she starts feeling dizzy is it pregnancy or something more serious?

The Producer's Unlikely Bride: What happens when a producer and an author agree to a fake relationship?

Ava's Blessing in Disguise: Five years after marriage, Ava faces a mysterious illness that threatens to ruin her career. Will she find out what it is?

The Soldier's Steadfast Bride: Heidi and Cory made a pact as kids. Will she honor it now if it means she might have to marry without love?

The Men of Fire Beach

Fire Games: Cassidy returns home from Who Wants to Marry a Cowboy to find obsessive letters from a fan. The cop assigned to help her wants to get back to his case, but what she sees at a fire may just be the key he's looking for.

Lost Memories and New Beginnings: A doctor, a patient with no memory, the men out to get her. Can he keep her safe when he doesn't know who he's looking for?

When Questions Abound: A Companion story to Lost Memories. Told from Detective Graves' point of view.

Never Forget the Past: Fireman Bubba must confront his past in order to clear his name and save lives.

Love on the Run: Graham is forced into lockdown with one of his employees. Will he be able to save her from her ex and will she steal his heart?

Secrets and Suspense: Cara Hunter is hiding something about her military past. When she's suspected of murder, will she be able to convince Cole she's the victim?

Rescue My Heart coming soon: Al's sister is missing. Can she find her in time?

The Men of Fire Beach Collection: Books 1-3

Texas Tornadoes

Defending My Heart: Forced to confront his past, Emmitt finds news that will change his life.

Run With My Heart: Sentenced to community service, Tucker finds himself falling for the manager.

Love on the Line: Blaine has hired Kenzi to redo his cabin, but what happens when she finds his darkest secret?

Touchdown on Love: When Mason's injury throws him together with ex-girlfriend, will sparks fly again?

Second Chance Reception: Jefferson is hiding something. When he falls for the team cook, will he let her in?

Small Town Short Stories

Small Town Dreams

Small Town Second Chances

Small Town Rivals

Small Town Life

Life in a Small Town: All four stories in one collection

Stand Alones:

Love Renewed: This books is part of the multi author second chance series. When fate reunites high school sweethearts separated by life's choices, can they find a second chance at love at a snowy lodge amid a little mystery?

Her children's early reader chapter book series:

The Wishing Stone #1: Dangerous Dinosaur

The Wishing Stone #2: Dragon Dilemma

The Wishing Stone #3: Mesmerizing Mermaids

The Wishing Stone #4: Pyramid Puzzle
The Wishing Stone: Mary's Miracle
The Wishing Stone #5: Superhero City
The Wishing Stone Collection
To see a list of all her books

authorloranahoopes.com
loranahoopes@gmail.com

ABOUT THE AUTHOR

Lorana Hoopes is an inspirational author originally from Texas but now living in the PNW with her husband and three children. When not writing, she can be seen kickboxing at the gym, singing, or acting on stage. One day, she hopes to retire from teaching and write full time.

www.ingramcontent.com/pod-product-compliance
Lightning Source LLC
Chambersburg PA
CBHW030303180626
46810CB00003B/905